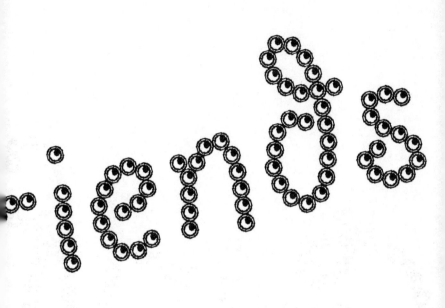

That night round the camp fire (most of which had been gathered by me) it was boys and girls all mixed up together. Chloë and I sat next to each other, but on her other side was the Gangle – and she paid far more attention to him than she did to me. On my other side I had a weepy Domenica, only she wasn't so weepy any more. She'd been on table-laying duty with the little weedy guy, and it seemed they'd hit it off together. Now they were buddies, and all matey-matey. Even Domenica didn't need me any more.

From that moment on, I just hated summer camp. Everything went wrong that possibly could.

Also by Jean Ure
in the Girlfriends series

Pink Knickers Aren't Cool!
Girls Stick Together!
Girls Are Groovy!

Orchard Black Apples

Get a Life
Just 16
Love is for Ever

ORCHARD BOOKS
96 Leonard Street
London EC2A 4XD
Orchard Books Australia
Unit 31/56 O'Riordan Street, Alexandria, NSW 2015
ISBN 1 84121 847 2
First published in Great Britain in 2002
A paperback original
Text © Jean Ure 2002
The right of Jean Ure to be identified as the author of
this work has been asserted by her in accordance with the
Copyright, Designs and Patents Act, 1988.
A CIP catalogue record for this book is available from the British Library.
1 3 5 7 9 10 8 6 4 2
Printed in Great Britain

Jean Ure

ORCHARD BOOKS

Chapter 1

"So, you guys!" Keri hoisted herself up onto my window ledge. "What gives?"

Lily and I looked at each other. I giggled; Lily pulled a face. Keri was at it again...trying to be oh, so cool!

She is quite cool, actually; but sometimes she just, like, overdoes it. And Frizz didn't understand her, anyway. In tones of puzzlement, she said, "*What gives?*"

"That's right, kiddo!" Keri punched the air. "What gives! Meaning," she added kindly, in normal everyday English, "what's new in your life?"

Keri was obviously in a good mood. Ordinarily she

would have got impatient, but today she was sounding well pleased with herself.

It was Saturday afternoon, and for once we had all turned up. Lily, Keri, Frizz and me. The Gang of Four! (Plus Bundle, who is my dog.) It was our last meeting before the summer holidays, so we'd all made an extra-special effort. Just recently, we'd had rather a lot of meetings where there'd only been three of us, or sometimes even just two. Once or twice we'd even had to cancel. It wasn't that we were losing interest, or stopping being friends, or anything like that; just that the summer term had been so-o-o busy.

For all of us! Even for Frizz, who had simply hated her first term at Heathfield. But she'd settled down, now, and made some friends, and even joined the drama club. I could hardly believe it! Frizz, joining the drama club! Frizz. Who used to be so shy she wouldn't even put up her hand in class to answer a question! She was really coming out of her shell.

It was since she'd won the Junior Schools Chef of the Year Competition and been on the telly and had her picture in all the local newspapers. It hadn't made her big-headed, because Frizz isn't like that, but it did seem to have given her lashings of confidence. Which was nice as it meant the rest of us didn't have to feel guilty when good things happened to us, such as, for example, me getting a poem in the school magazine, or Keri scoring goals in a hockey match, or Lily being chosen for special dance classes. That sort of thing. We didn't have to feel responsible. Before it had always been, "What about Frizz? Poor old Frizz!" She wasn't poor old Frizz any more and it was a great weight off our minds.

Plus, of course, we were genuinely happy for her. And proud! I'd told everyone at school, "That was my friend Frizz on the telly." I couldn't help doing a little bit of boasting. I was friends with a celeb!

Lily is another celeb, or is going to be. She is going to be a famous dancer and people the world over will drink champagne from her ballet shoes. (Pink satin, natch!) Frizz is going to be a famous chef and have her own restaurant (*cordon vert*, which means veggie) and Keri is just going to be Keri (and will probably be famous just for that). I don't yet know what I am going to be. Whatever it is, I don't expect I shall be famous. Boo hoo! But I don't really mind. When you are little and round – well, roundish – you are probably not cut out for fame. And anyway, what a drag! People wanting your autograph all the time, and recognising you wherever you go. I especially wouldn't want to be recognised when I am taking Bundle round the park, as I am usually to be seen in a disgusting old anorak and muddy wellies. "Yeeurgh! Look!" (People would go.) "That's Polly Roberts... What a sight!"

So I think I'll just stay anonymous, and let the rest of them twinkle and shine. It doesn't bother me one little bit!

I beamed round at them as they sat there in my bedroom – Keri perched on the window ledge, with her feet propped on a chair, Lily cross-legged on the floor and Frizz flopped on the bed, with Bundle stretched out beside her. These were my friends! My very best friends, that I'd known since way back. Year Two, Year Three. We'd all been at different schools since September. Lily was at her dancing school, Frizz was at Heathfield, Keri (whose mum and dad are seriously rich) at her posh boarding school and me at the High School, which Frizz calls the Boffin School.

My mum and dad are not seriously rich, since money does not, as Mum is forever telling me, grow on trees, so I'd had to get a scholarship, which was what made Frizz call me Boffin Head, which I used to wish she wouldn't. She doesn't do it so much any more; she stopped after she became a celeb. It was like, now we were equals. I was a boffin head; she was a celeb!

We'd all made this vow, before we left Juniors, that we'd still go on being the Gang of Four. We were going to meet up every Saturday, taking it in turns whose place we'd go to. And we had! All through the winter term, all through the spring term, all through the summer. But now it was holidays, which meant this might be our last meeting for a while. Which was why we'd all made an effort and turned up.

"So, you guys!" That was Keri, leaning forward on her window ledge (and nearly overbalancing). "What's new?" Keri hadn't been at the last meeting; she'd gone off to do things with her friend Jemima. "What's been happening?"

"We've broken up," said Frizz. "Two months of freedom, yum yum yum!"

"Utter bliss," agreed Keri.

"I've got stuff to do," I said. "Simply masses of it!"

"Stuff?" said Keri. "What sort of stuff?"

"Essays and stuff. Summer homework."

Frizz pulled a face and said, "Boffin school!"

I told her that I didn't really mind. "I quite like working."

Frizz and Keri looked at each other and shook their heads. Which was something they'd never have done before Frizz became a celeb.

"Well, whatever turns you on," drawled Keri.

Lily piped up from the floor (where she was busy contorting herself into odd shapes). "I still have to practise every day."

"Oh. Well! You," said Keri. "You're a dancer. That's different."

I didn't quite see why. Lily has to exercise her body, I have to exercise my mind; Lily likes stretching and bending, I like reading and writing. Why should Keri sneer at me and not at Lily? 'Cos I knew that was what she was doing. Oh, Polly. She's just a boffin. It really annoys me! But I didn't say anything 'cos of it being our last meeting until (probably) next term. I didn't want to make waves or anything.

"So where's everybody going?" said Keri. "What's everybody's plans?" She was just dying to tell us hers!

"Go on," I said. "What are yours?"

"Well—" Keri tried to hug her knees up to her chin and nearly slipped off the window ledge. It's not really wide enough for sitting on. Her feet fell back on the chair with a hasty plonk. "First I'm going off to stay with Mima for a couple of weeks. We're going to ride like crazy! All day every day! I'm taking Clancy with me."

By Mima she meant her friend Jemima. By Clancy she meant her new pony. She'd only had him a few weeks, so naturally she was quite excited still and couldn't stop talking about him. We'd all been to visit him in his field, and Lily (who is braver than me and Frizz) had been for a bit of a ride on him. Me and Frizz had just stroked his darling velvety nose and fed him carrots. He is a very sweet-natured pony and Keri loves him to bits. She has sworn that even when she grows too big for him she won't sell him but will keep him for always. She says it is just too horrid when people get rid of their ponies.

Although at times Keri can be absolutely maddening, there are lots and lots of good things about her. Which is why we are friends! But she can be maddening, all the same.

"After I've visited Mima, we're flying over to the States." She announced it like anyone else might say they were going to Brighton, or down to Cornwall. She wasn't showing off. Not exactly. Probably, to her, it just seemed a normal everyday sort of thing to do.

"First we're stopping off in New York," gushed Keri. "Then we're going on to Boston. Then we're spending the rest of the time in this place called Cape Cod."

There was a pause, while we digested all this to-ing and fro-ing. Then Frizz giggled and said, "I'm going to this place called Cooden Beach."

Cooden Beach is where her granny lives, in a bungalow. It is near Eastbourne, where loads of grannies live. Whenever I have been there with Frizz it is always full of very ancient sort of people. At least, that is how it seems to me.

"Cooden Beach," said Frizz. "You know?"

The way she said it was like really cool. Lily cackled, with one leg twisted round the back of her head. (Don't ask me how she gets into these positions. It's like she's made of rubber, or something.) I sort of twitched my lips but didn't actually giggle. Not that I didn't think it funny, but – well! The reason I didn't giggle will become clear in a moment or two.

"There is absolutely nothing wrong," said Keri, "with holidaying in England." And she smiled kindly at Frizz as she said it. Oh, dear! I told you she can be infuriating. She is one of those people, it is next to impossible to snub. (Mainly because she never recognises that you are doing it.)

"I am sure," said Keri, "that it is very patriotic to holiday in England. It is just – you know!" She simpered. "We have these relatives over *there*."

There was a bit of a silence after she said this. Frizz cuddled with Bundle, Lily unwrapped her leg, I sat down at my workstation and frowned at my diary. My diary is where I write down all my (ahem!) social engagements. I knew what I had written in there. No one else did. Not yet. Not even Frizz.

"So what about Lily?" said Keri. "What is she doing? Hey! You!" she said, poking at Lily with a foot.

"Me?" Lily rocketed into a sitting position. A big goofy beam spread across her face. "I'm going to summer school!"

"School! Ugh!" Frizz crinkled her nose.

"No, I'm really looking forward to it," said Lily.

She'd been given a place at this special summer dance school and was going to spend the whole of August doing exactly what she'd just spent the whole of April, May and June doing...bending, stretching, twisting, jumping. Wearing herself to a frazzle. She just couldn't wait to get started!

"Some holiday," I said.

"No, it will be," insisted Lily. "It's going to be brilliant! It's in a great big old house, and we're all going to stay there. Just like boarding school! We're going down in a coach, all the way to Devon."

"Devon," said Frizz. "Cream teas! Scrummy!" But mentioning cream teas to a dancer is like mentioning veal to a veggie. (Actually, I am not a veggie – quite – but I certainly wouldn't eat veal. I think anyone that eats veal is the pits.)

Lily screamed and collapsed in a heap, where she lay moaning dramatically. "Fat, fat, fat!"

It is a sort of joke with us, the idea of Lily getting fat. She is skinny as a matchstick.

"I would guzzle cream teas all day long if I were going to Devon," said Frizz.

"Yes, well, you're not," said Keri. "You're going to Cooden Beach. And just as well!" she added. "You'd come back like a great puffball."

"Wouldn't worry me," boasted Frizz.

She had become very bold since being on telly. She spoke back to Keri all of the time! When we were at Juniors she wouldn't have dared. But it is good. More people, I think, should speak back to Keri. I do myself quite often, even though I am not a celeb.

"So! That's me going to America." Keri counted off on her fingers. "Lily going to Devon. Frizz going to Cooden Beach – grooving with granny!" Keri swung her hips to and fro (as best she could, without slipping off the window ledge). "I guess Polly will be going as well?"

This was the moment I'd been dreading. Well, perhaps not dreading, but I had definitely been feeling a bit anxious. See, for the last two years I had gone with Frizz. What happened, her mum would drive us both down there – me and Frizz, and Bundle, 'cos he likes holidays as much as anyone. Then Frizz's mum would come back home, to help Frizz's dad in their newsagent's shop, and two weeks later she'd come and pick us up again. We'd spend most of the time on the beach, or mooching round town, or sometimes Frizz's granny would take us out for the day. It wasn't what you'd call exciting, but it was fun.

Better than staying at home! Which is what would have happened otherwise. My mum and dad hardly ever get away in the summer months because of Dad's work. He puts swimming pools in for people, and also does odd jobs such as building walls and painting houses. Summer is one of his busiest times. So up until now I'd always been really grateful that I could go with Frizz to Cooden Beach. It was just that this time…

I swallowed. I could feel Frizz looking at me, like she was already picking up the vibes.

"Grrrrooooving," said Keri, "with grrrrannnny!" And this time she slipped right off the window ledge, and serve her right.

"You are going to come, aren't you?" said Frizz.

"Well, er, mm, ah, the thing is," I gabbled, "there's this summer camp thing, the whole of August, and I

19

just couldn't get out of it, you know what it's like, when your mum wants you to do something, and poooor Bundle!" I crooned. "He won't be able to come with me, poor little man! He won't have a holiday! I'd ever so much rather come with you," I told Frizz, "but Mum's gone and arranged it all, I mean she's paid the money and everything, it's just so annoying!"

"Summer camp sounds great," said Keri. "Where is it?"

"Er, mm, Dorking," I said. "Near Dorking!"

"Lots of good riding country, near Dorking," said Keri.

"Yes, I know," I said. I did my best to sound really miserable. "I'm going to have to go pony trekking."

I rolled my eyes, and Lily promptly collapsed with her legs in the air.

"Pony trekking! And you wouldn't even walk round the field on Clancy!"

"Oh, don't worry," said Keri. "They wouldn't put you on a pony like Clancy. They'll all be neddies. Like perambulating armchairs. You couldn't fall off if you tried!"

I said, "I bet I do!" I just said it, really, to make Frizz feel better. I didn't want her thinking that I was, like, eager. I mean, I was, 'cos it was all untrue about Mum forcing me, I'd actually begged and pleaded with her to let me go. But I didn't want to upset Frizz more than I had to. I just knew that if I looked in her direction I'd find her eyes all big and soulful, fixed on me.

Keri was already launched on horsey talk, telling me how I'd have to wear a hard hat so that even if I did come off I wouldn't hurt myself, and in any case it all happened so fast, if it did happen, you hardly had time to be scared, but one thing I'd got to remember, and that was at all costs, hold on to the reins. "'Cos if you don't the horse might go galloping off and that would be a great nuisance and not only ruin your ride but everyone else's ride, too. And you wouldn't want to do that," said Keri.

"I don't really want to do it at all," I said, crossing my fingers behind my back.

"No, you'll enjoy it!" cried Keri. "Let's all promise to send postcards so they'll be waiting for us when we get back!"

I'd been hoping – I am such a coward – that Frizz's mum or dad would come to pick her up before Keri's mum came for Lily and Keri, but of course they didn't. Keri's mum arrived, and Keri and Lily went off, promising to send postcards, and I was left on my own with Frizz.

"You might have told me," she said.

"I'm sorry! I only knew just a few days ago. I

mean…" I waved a hand. What did I mean? What I meant was that I'd been putting it off and putting it off until it couldn't be put off any longer. "I'd have asked you to come, too, only I knew you'd be going to your gran's!"

"I don't have to go to my gran's," said Frizz.

"Well, n-no, but –"

I was going with Chloë! My best friend at school. Chloë was my school best friend; Frizz was my out-of-school one. Mum had said why didn't I ask Dawn (this is Frizz's real name) if she'd like to go with us. How could I explain to Mum that it either had to be me-and-Frizz or me-and-Chloë? It couldn't be me-and-Chloë-and-Frizz. It just wouldn't work. Mum would immediately have said, "Why not?" but I didn't know why not! It was just something I instinctively felt.

So I'd mumbled about Frizz's mum and dad maybe not being able to afford it, and Mum had been forced to admit that that might be true. Once at Juniors Frizz hadn't been able to go on a school trip because her mum and dad didn't have enough money. They are quite poor, I think. Frizz has sometimes had to wear clothes from charity shops, which I would hate to have to do. I am not quite sure why they are so poor but it is something to do with a big supermarket taking away all their business, which I think is so sad.

Anyway, Mum said it was a shame, because it would have been fun if the three of us could all have gone to camp together. She didn't understand! Chloë had invited me. She hadn't invited Frizz!

I felt sorry if Frizz was upset, but it wasn't as if we had actually positively arranged anything. It wasn't like I'd said that I was going. It was just something that she'd taken for granted. And anyway, Frizz was a celeb, so I didn't feel too bad.

I said, "Look, we'll see each other before I leave!"

"When?" said Frizz.

"Next week?"

"Which day?"

I said, "I'll give you a ring! Or you ring me."

"All right," said Frizz.

I knew she thought that I'd let her down, but heavens! I mean. She'd made new friends, I'd made new friends. I didn't get all worked up and jealous about hers. Not that I'd told her I was going with Chloë but that was because I knew, if I had done, she would have gone even more reproachful than she already was. She would have made me feel like a traitor.

All I'm saying, I didn't think people ought to take things for granted. That's all.

Chapter 2

I didn't get to see Frizz again before I went to camp.
It wasn't my fault! First off, she didn't ring me until
Wednesday. In the evening. She wanted us to go into
town together on Friday, but I couldn't 'cos we were
all going off – me and Bundle, and Mum and Dad, and
Craig (he's my brother) to visit my auntie for the
weekend.

I said, "We won't be back till Monday."

Frizz said, "Oh."

I told her that I could do it on Thursday, but she
said Thursday wasn't any good. She didn't say why it

wasn't any good, and I couldn't think what else she would be doing as Frizz does not have what I would describe as a mad social life. (Neither do I, to be honest; not like Keri, who has all these stacks and stacks of friends that she visits with and does things with and goes places with.)

Frizz wanted to know, what about next week? I said that I would have to check my diary. "Hang on! I'll just have a look and see what it says."

So I looked, and it didn't say anything at all (which it mostly doesn't, but I like to pretend). I told Frizz that I could do "any day except Friday", because I thought that on Friday I would be busy packing my bags for camp.

Frizz said, "Tuesday?"

I said Tuesday would be OK and I made a big note in my diary – MEET FRIZZ – and underlined it, twice.

"I'll ring you," said Frizz, "and we can arrange a time."

Well! Guess what? She rings me on Monday, just after we've got back from my auntie's, to say she'd forgotten that she was "doing something" on Tuesday.

"Can you manage Wednesday?"

I said no, I couldn't. "I'm doing something!"

It was true. I wasn't just making it up in a fit of crossness. Chloë had asked me if I'd go shopping with her. She wanted to buy stuff for camp. Tops, and trainers, and stuff.

"I could manage Thursday," I said.

"I can't Thursday!" wailed Frizz. "I'm going to the dentist!"

"What, all day?" I said.

"No, but Mum's going to take me to have my hair cut afterwards."

"Oh ho! Really short?" I said.

"N-no. I don't think so." Frizz sounded as if she didn't quite know what she was going to have done. "Just sort of…tidied up. Ready for going away."

I felt like saying, "But you're only going to your gran's!" I mean, who did she think she was going to meet? In Cooden Beach???

I didn't say it, 'cos it would have been unkind. Frizz is very sensitive about her hair. It's pale, and rather wispy. Keri (our style queen!) was forever nagging at her to "get something done with it". I just didn't want her thinking it was my fault if we didn't get to meet, is all. I wasn't the one who'd muddled my engagements! And what engagements, anyway? Frizz was becoming more and more secretive. When she'd won the cooking competition she hadn't even told us that she was going in for it! Now she was off doing other things with other people instead of meeting up with me, her oldest friend.

I started to get a bit resentful until I remembered that I was meeting up with Chloë – I was even going to summer camp with Chloë – so I couldn't really get too mad at her. But it wasn't like Frizz. Frizz didn't do things with other people!

She said miserably that she supposed now we wouldn't see each other again until I came back from Dorking.

"Unless you got your hair cut on Friday?" I said.

"I can't! Mum's gone and made the appointment. She's having hers done, too. I wish you were coming to Gran's with me!"

"I know." I sighed. "I'm dreading it!"

"Send me a postcard," said Frizz.

I promised that I would. "And we'll meet up when I get back!"

I wasn't really dreading camp. I was looking forward to it! I was excited! A whole month away from home! And with Chloë, who I got on really well with. We didn't know each other's secrets, like me and Frizz did – well, like me and Frizz used to do, before she became a celeb – but we shared jokes and we giggled at the same sort of thing. So I knew it would be fun.

On Wednesday, Chloë and I went shopping together. Mum told me I could buy myself "Whatever you want, up to £25", so I got:

a vest top
a pair of stripy socks
some coloured bangles
a hair slide shaped like a butterfly
a pair of sunglasses
two lots of stick-on tattoos
some sequin patches
a mobile phone carrier
and a special embroidered bag to put everything in.
Phew! A lot of shopping!

I rushed back home to show it all to Mum. Craig was there and said, "What a stupid waste of money! You're only going to camp."

"I need all these things," I said. "And anyway, they didn't come to half as much as your Playstation! Didn't even come to a quarter as much. Didn't even come to…"

"To what?" said Craig.

To whatever was smaller than a quarter! (I am not very good at Maths.)

"Didn't even come to a crumb!"

"Shouldn't think it did," said Craig. "That stuff's all junk."

"It is not!" I screeched. I am always screeching at Craig. He provokes me.

"Course it is," he said. "Girls always buy junk!"

"We do not!"

"Yes, you do! You buy tat!"

I was about to fly at him and gouge both his eyes out when Mum stepped in. As usual!

"I must say," she said, "that it will be extremely peaceful in this house when you have both gone."

Craig was also going off to camp. A different one from mine, thank goodness! He was going with his friend Jobsy (Kevin Jobson, a boy in his class at school). I pitied any poor girls that were going to be there.

"I do hope," I said to Mum, as she drove me round to Chloë's on Saturday morning, "there won't be any boys where I'm going."

"Oh, I should think there will be," said Mum. "It's not single sex, as far as I know."

"But we won't have to...do things together?" I said.

Mum laughed. "It depends what sort of things! I'm sure you'll eat together and play games together, and go trekking. That sort of thing."

"We won't have to sleep in the same room?"

This was something that hadn't occurred to me (up until now). The idea of sleeping in the same hut with a load of boys! I didn't even have pyjamas or a nightie; just a T-shirt and pants. I would die. Mum, however, assured me that we would have separate sleeping quarters, so after that I stopped worrying. Chloë and I would stick together. We wouldn't want anything to do with boys!

The first day at camp was ace. I really thought that I was going to love it. There weren't that many of us, just ten boys and ten girls, which is nicer (I think) than vast hordes. It means you can feel all cosy and get to know each other. Not that I particularly wanted to get to know any boys, but you have to be a bit friendly. You have to be polite; you can't just ignore them. They are people the same as the rest of us, and have their feelings, even though it doesn't always seem like it.

That first day was spent settling in. People kept arriving all morning with their mums and dads. The camp leaders, Pete and Geri, would go up and greet them, and introduce them to the rest of us, and show them where they were going to sleep, and where they could stash all their stuff, etc. Me and Chloë were two of the first to arrive, and get settled in.

The camp consisted of three huts, down in a big

hollow surrounded by trees. Just as Mum had promised, the boys slept in one hut and the girls in another, in bunk beds, of which Chloë bagged a top one 'cos she said she was always scared, if she was at the bottom, that the one above would collapse on her. This is not one of my great fears, so I took the one underneath.

The third hut was the biggest, and that was for eating in, and for playing indoor games in, if, for instance, the weather was bad.

Me and Chloë stuck together that first day, just like I'd imagined we would. We talked to other people, of course, but we sat together when it came to chow time (which is what Pete and Geri called meal times) and we put our names down for the same activities, like you got a choice each day (Sunday's for instance being hiking or orienteering, of which we chose hiking) and when the duty roster was posted we were down for the same chores, examples of which were: preparing food, laying tables, washing up, collecting firewood, and so on.

That Saturday we got to help prepare food, which was all veggie, which made some people – mostly the boys – groan and pull faces, but Pete said, "We don't eat animals here", and I must say that I approved. I thought that when I got home I would suggest to Mum that maybe I should stop eating animals, too. I didn't think, actually, if they hadn't been told, that the boys would have noticed the sausages weren't made of murdered pig but were in fact vegebangers. They just made a fuss 'cos they thought it was macho. Me and Chloë agreed that "that was boys for you". I was so glad she felt the same way I did!

After supper we all sat round a camp fire and sang songs, accompanied by Pete on the guitar. That was brilliant! I do not have a very tuneful voice and would be far too terrified to sing on my own, but with other people it is all right. Nobody notices if you keep hitting wrong notes.

That first night the boys mostly sat on one side and the girls on the other. It just happened that way. Nobody said, "Boys over there, girls over here." Geri teased us and said, "We'll have you mingling before very long!" But I didn't think so.

We didn't go to bed till really late. There was one girl, Domenica, that had the bunk opposite mine, that was homesick and started to cry very quietly to herself after everyone else had gone to sleep. Everyone except me! You could tell the others were asleep from the way they breathed, quite heavy and with little whiffles and grunts. She probably thought nobody would hear her, but I was lying awake going over the events of the day and writing postcards in my head, thinking what I would say to the others, and especially Frizz.

Camp isn't nearly as bad as I thought it was going to be! We have all eaten vegebangers and had a sing-song round the fire. It is good fun.

And then I would add something about still wishing I could be with her at her granny's, so that she wouldn't feel I was enjoying myself too much without her.

I was trying to work out the words in my head when I heard the sound of muffled weeping and knew that it was Domenica. She'd been a bit pale and watery all day, and earlier on I'd seen her tearfully clinging to her mum when her mum was trying to leave. So I heaved myself out of my bunk and crouched down beside her and asked her what the matter was. Between sniffles she told me that she hadn't wanted to come, she'd never been away from home before, not even for a single day, and she didn't know how she was going to survive for four whole weeks. She added that she hadn't realised there were going to be boys. "Mum never told me!" She said that she was an only child and went to an all-girls' school and had practically never even spoken to a boy before. I said that I, unfortunately, had to speak to boys all of the time – well, one boy. Craig, my brother! I said, "Believe me, that is quite enough", and she actually giggled so I guessed that she was already starting to feel a bit better and I crawled back into my bunk intending to go on with my postcards, except that by then I was so tired that I immediately fell asleep and knew no more till morning.

So! That was Day One. A really good day. It was on Day Two that it all started to go wrong. It began OK. We all went into the mess hut for chow, then Pete and Geri handed out lunch packs and we divided into two groups, those that were going on a hike and those that were going to orienteer. Most of the boys, for some reason, had chosen to go orienteering. Only two came on the hike. A great gangling thing with red hair, and a little weedy one with spots.

I felt a bit sorry for the weedy one, even though he was a boy. I thought it must be horrid to have spots, and also he was shy and kept going bright red every time anyone spoke to him. This is something that I myself do rather a lot, so that I thought perhaps I would make an effort to be friendly, only Chloë grabbed me by the arm and hissed, "Stick together!" so we did, and spent most of our time making jokes and giggling. We always find lots to giggle about. Domenica, still a bit sniffly and puffy round the eyes, tagged along with us, but we didn't mind her being there. It was just those boys we didn't want!

We were all rather tired when we got back from the hike, but there is no rest for the wicked (as one of my grans is fond of saying). Me and Chloë were down for "Firewood Duty"…

Pete clapped his hands and said "Chop chop!", which I thought meant that we were going to take axes and chop down trees. In worried tones I said, "Is it all right to do that?"

Everyone looked at me as if I was mad. Pete said, "Do what?" I said, "Chop down trees", and they all hooted. I'd made an idiot of myself! Apparently when someone says "chop chop" it just means "hurry up" or "get a move on". Don't ask me why 'cos I haven't the faintest idea. How come everybody else always knows these things and not me??? It is so humiliating.

"Off you go," said Geri. "Quick march! Just remember…no wood, no fire!"

So off we dragged our weary bodies. There were five of us; me and Chloë, the Gangle, a girl called Saffy, which I think was short for Sapphire, and a boy who had the brightest blue eyes I have ever seen and was called Ryan. We clambered up out of the hollow and set off down the lane to look for wood. And that was when everything started to get horrid. Ryan and Gangle were still sniggering about me not knowing what "chop chop" meant. They kept going, "*Chop! Crash!*" and swinging imaginary axes at the trees.

"*Chop! Crash!* There goes another one!"

Needless to say, Chloë and Saffy started sniggering as well, which made me feel about six years old. At first I was glad when Ryan and Saffy peeled off together as I thought it meant that the sniggering would stop. Which it did, but then something worse happened: the Gangle started coming on to Chloë! And instead of telling him to stop being so pathetic, or even just ignoring him, Chloë played up to it. She kept giggling and simpering and doing this thing with her eyes, making them go all sort of big and surprised. I couldn't believe it! Chloë doing a girly routine! Chloë – who'd said we'd got to stick together!

Well. I kept my side of the bargain but she didn't keep hers. She not only unstuck herself (from me, I mean), she actually went off and left me on my own. One minute I was bending down picking up bits of wood, and she and the Gangle were mucking around doing their flirty thing, the next minute I was straightening up and looking round for them and they'd gone! I had a moment of panic 'cos to be honest I don't have very much sense of direction and I thought that on my own I might be lost. I might not know how to get back again! They would have to send out a search party, and then I would feel even more humiliated than I already did.

And then I heard crashing sounds, and the bushes burst apart and Chloë came running out, screeching. Screeching and giggling, both at the same time. The Gangle came running after, waving something in the air. Ugh! It was a rabbit's paw. Some poor little rabbit had obviously been nobbled. I hoped that it was a fox that had got it, and not some horrible trap. I hate it so much when people use traps! I think it is so cruel. Not that the Gangle would have cared. He obviously had no feelings.

Chloë was shrieking at the top of her voice. "Geroff! Geroff!" But you could tell that really and truly she was enjoying it. She liked him chasing after her with a rabbit's paw!

That night round the camp fire (most of which had been gathered by me) it was boys and girls all mixed up together. Chloë and I sat next to each other, but on her other side was the Gangle – and she paid far more attention to him than she did to me. On my other side I had a weepy Domenica, only she wasn't so weepy any more. She'd been on table-laying duty with the little weedy guy, and it seemed they'd hit it off together. Now they were buddies, and all matey-matey. Even Domenica didn't need me any more.

From that moment on, I just hated summer camp. Everything went wrong that possibly could.

On Monday we went pony trekking and I fell off, which was the thing Keri had said it would be impossible to do. Well, she was wrong, 'cos I did! And while I was picking myself up, and trying not to cry (which would have been just too babyish for words) Chloë went jogging on with the Gangle to the head of the line, leaving me to trail dismally by myself at the rear.

Another day we went orienteering, which we had to do in pairs, and I was so utterly useless that Chloë said next time would I mind awfully if she did it with the Gangle, instead?

I said, "You can do it with whoever you like," and she said, "Oh, Polly, please don't be mad at me! It's just that..." and then she had the nerve to giggle. "It's like trying to find your way with a blind worm!"

To which I retorted, "That is a very blind wormist remark", hoping that she would feel rebuked, but she just giggled all the more, as if I had said something amusing.

The only thing I was any good at was telling creepy stories round the camp fire. I am good at creepy stories! I can make them really sssssssspine-chilling. But all the time, out of the corner of my eye, I could see Chloë clutching at the Gangle in mock terror. They just took every opportunity to grab at each other. So disgusting! I couldn't imagine what she saw in him. Saffy and Ryan were almost as bad, but at least Ryan had these gorgeous blue eyes and was quite hunky altogether. Whereas the Gangle was just…gangly! Plus he had red hair. Keri also has red hair, but hers is deep and dark and glowing. The Gangle's was like carrots. Which are not one of my favourite vegetables!

I had never thought that Chloë would go goo-goo-eyed over a boy. She'd always been so bright and sparky and funny. We'd always giggled together at the same jokes. Now she giggled with the Gangle and seemed to have lost all interest in me.

I suppose, to be fair, she did try. To include me, I mean. The Gangle had this friend called Robbo and Chloë kept pretending that he was interested in me. But I knew that he wasn't. I wasn't interested in him, either. We both went bright red whenever we were together. It was just so embarrassing! I mean, we just didn't have a single thing to talk about. So in the end Chloë gave up and Robbo went off with the other boys and I was left on my own.

It is horrid being the odd one out. I just couldn't find anyone to bond with! Sometimes I dragged along with Chloë and the Gangle and felt like a raspberry, or a gooseberry, or whatever it is. Sometimes I hung around with Domenica, or with Domenica and the little weedy guy, whose name was Joseph. They didn't make me feel like a raspberry (or a gooseberry) but they were both very young for their ages. They were in any case younger than me as they were only ten, whereas I was twelve, which is practically teenage. When I wasn't hanging with them I just mooched dismally by myself, counting the days till the torture would end.

I sent postcards to the others. I told Lily and Keri that I was having a brilliant time (there is such a thing as pride) but to Frizz, because she is my oldest friend, I confessed the truth:

I hate pony trekking and orienteering and being with loads of people. I would ever so much rather have gone with you to visit your gran.

I just couldn't wait to get back!

Chapter 3

The day Mum came to take me away from that camp was the best day of my entire whole life. I was just so glad to be home. I was so happy to see everyone! Mum and Dad. Bundle. Even (almost) Craig! Which goes to show how much I had been suffering. I mean, for me to be happy at seeing Craig...well! It speaks for itself, I rather think.

The first thing I did, after rolling about the floor with Bundle, was rush to the phone and ring Frizz. I just wanted to hear the sound of her voice and pour out my woes. I wanted to say how much I'd missed her and have her say how much she'd missed me. But Frizz wasn't there! Her mum said, "Oh, Polly! I'm afraid you're out of luck. She's gone off for the day with a friend, she won't be back till quite late. Shall I get her to give you a call in the morning?"

I said yes please and put the phone down feeling both miffed and miserable. I knew I didn't have any right to feel miffed, but that just made me feel more miffed than ever. Miffed with me more than with Frizz! Frizz hadn't done anything wrong. I was the one that had done something wrong, or at any rate stupid, going off with Chloë to have a perfectly hateful time when I could have been with Frizz, enjoying myself.

"Did you see all your postcards?" said Mum. "Look! Four of them."

I said, "Four?" thinking, who could have sent the extra one?

It was Keri. There was one from Lily, one from Frizz, and there were two from Keri. Keri was having what she called a "super mega hyper brilliant time". In her first card she said that "America is heaven and I am in bliss!" In her second card she said that "America is bliss and I am in heaven!" Neat, or what???

Mum said, "Is that from Keri? Is she enjoying herself?"

"I guess so," I said.

Lily had sent me a picture of a load of old ruins. On the back she had written, "This is ME. Old ruin! I am *dissintergrating*." (Lily has never been any good at spelling.) "We are working very hard and are being forced to eat a lot of callries" (heavens! You would think she could at least spell *calories*) "to keep our weight up. I am getting F.A.T."

Oh, yes? I'd like to see it!

Frizz's card was the seafront at Eastbourne. The seafront that was always full of old people, where I could have been with Frizz, feeling happy and secure and not troubled by boys.

On the back, in large sprawly letters that took up practically the whole of the card, Frizz had written: "The weather is good. I have been in the water three times. Tomorrow we are going on a coach trip. Lots of love, Frizz."

I thought, disgruntledly, that she might have found a bit more to say. She might, for instance, have said that she was missing me, or wished that I was there. That is what I had said on my card. Also, when I write postcards I bunch my words up really small so that I can get a lot on, otherwise what is the point? But Frizz is a cook, like Lily is a dancer. They are not word people.

I tried ringing the other two just in case they were back, but at Keri's no one answered and Lily's dad said that Lily wouldn't be home until next week, so there wasn't anyone I could speak to. Instead I had to spend the evening listening to Craig relating in boring detail all the things that he had done while he had been at his camp. After a bit Dad said, "What about you, Poll Doll? What sort of things did you get up to?"

"Nothing very much," I said.

"Didn't you enjoy it?" said Mum.

I wanted so much just to rush at her and bury my head and burst into tears, like I did when I was little. I wanted to tell her how horrid it had been. How boys had ruined everything and taken Chloë away from me and left me on my own and how I was just never ever going to fit in. But of course I couldn't. Partly because Craig was there, and partly because I was twelve years old and you just don't do that sort of thing when you are twelve years old. So I put on a brave face and said, "It was OK."

"You're just not a sporty outdoor type," said Mum. "What would probably suit you better would be a summer school of some kind. Something structured."

I thought that what would suit me better was just being on my own with Frizz. Next year when she invited me to Cooden Beach I would say yes! I was never ever going to go to summer camp again.

In the morning I waited anxiously for Frizz to call me. I didn't like to call her, I don't know why. I mean, there wasn't any reason that I shouldn't. It was just – well! I thought it might seem a bit eager.

The phone rang just as we were finishing breakfast. I leapt into the hall and clawed up the receiver before Craig could get to it. Breathlessly I said, "Hello?"

Frizz's voice came clattering joyously down the line. "Pollee! You're back!"

We arranged to meet that same afternoon. I said that I would go round to Frizz's place, and Mum said she would drop me off and that Dad could pick me up later, on his way home. "You're bound to want a bit of time, to catch up with each other."

I was quite surprised when I saw Frizz. She'd had her hair styled! Usually it is just long and straggly, but she'd had it layered, or feathered, or razored, or something. Well, anyway, shaped. (I am not an expert on hair. Mine is just short and clumpy.)

"Hey!" I cried. "That looks really cool!"

A big beam spread itself across Frizz's face. "D'you think so?"

I said, "Yeah, man! It's great!" (I don't normally talk this way, but it was how Craig had started talking since coming back from camp. It was catching.) "No, honest," I said, "it really suits you."

"D'you think Keri'll approve?" said Frizz. But I noticed that she didn't say it in her usual nervous tone of apprehension but more, like…so what if she doesn't? Who cares?

I said, "We cannot be dictated to by Keri."

Frizz said, "Right! She doesn't know everything. She just thinks she does!" Then she hooked her arm through mine and said, "Come upstairs and talk!"

Frizz's bedroom is way up in the roof, a teensy tiny little attic at the top of these really narrow stairs. We crammed up them together, trying to do it side by side as we did when we were small, and giggling when we got stuck. This was like old times! I was feeling happier already.

We threw ourselves on to Frizz's bed and settled in for a good long gossiping session. Frizz wanted to know what it had been like at camp. I told her the truth. I said, "It was perfectly horrid. I hated it!"

"Oh, poor you!" said Frizz. "What was so horrible?"

I said, "Everything! But mainly boys."

"Boys?" Frizz widened her eyes. "What was wrong with them?"

"Nothing specially. I mean, they were just boys. But they ruin things!"

Frizz crinkled her nose. "How d'you mean?"

"Well," I said, "f'r instance…some girls get really stupid when there's boys around. They get all gooey and smoochy. They go brain dead."

Frizz giggled.

"It's not funny," I said. "It's pathetic!"

Hastily, Frizz rearranged her features.

"If you'd been there," I said, "you'd know what I'm talking about. Anyway, I've had enough of summer camp. It was the hatefullest time I've ever had! I just want to forget all about it. Tell me about you! What was it like at your gran's?"

"Oh. Well! Yes. It was OK," said Frizz. "It would have been nicer if you'd been there, but we did lots of things. We went out on a boat and we did some day trips to places…oh, and there was an adventure playground! I know it sounds a bit babyish but there were lots of older kids there. We made up teams and played basketball, and rode BMXs round an obstacle course."

I was knocked out at the thought of Frizz, who is

just, like, totally unathletic, playing basketball and riding a BMX.

"I didn't know you could ride a bike," I said.

"I couldn't," said Frizz, "but I can now! Marigold said I had to learn." And then she went a bit pink, as if she'd said something she shouldn't have.

I said, "Marigold?"

"Marigold Johnson," said Frizz. "My friend at school."

"What, you mean she was down there?"

Frizz swallowed. "She came with me."

I said, "Oh."

"Well, you said you couldn't," said Frizz, "so I asked her, instead."

I expect I should immediately have said, "That's all right", or "You don't have to apologise", or "I'm glad you had someone to keep you company." Something cool and gracious, to show that I wasn't resentful. And certainly not jealous. Jealous of Marigold Johnson? Marigold, that used to be at Juniors? Ho, dear, no!

In fact, I didn't say anything at all, mainly because at the time I couldn't actually think of anything. And while I was still opening and shutting my mouth like a goldfish, and Frizz was growing pinker by the second, her mum calls up the attic stairs, "Dawn! Telephone!" and Frizz goes cantering gratefully off, leaving me to get on with my goldfish impersonation. Blob-pop-blobble-pop.

It does come as a bit of a shock when your best and oldest friend casually informs you that she's been on holiday with someone else, playing basketball and BMXing and going out on boats, having a simply wonderful time, while you've been at summer camp, hating every minute of it. Even if it is all your own fault.

Frizz was on the phone for simply ages. In the end I got curious and tiptoed on to the landing and hung over the banisters, trying to hear who she was talking to. I don't mean that I wanted to listen to her conversation; I wouldn't do a thing like that. I just wanted to find out if it was Marigold Johnson. As it happened, I couldn't make out anything that she was saying; all I could really hear was the sound of giggling. But it told me what I wanted to know: Marigold Johnson for sure. I went back to the bedroom and sat glumly on the bed, waiting for Frizz to return. When she did, she was all bright-eyed, all fizzing and bubbling.

"Who was that?" I said.

Frizz said, "Oh, just someone from school."

"Marigold?"

"No, Marigold's gone off with her mum and dad."

"Another holiday?" I said, wondering to myself who it could have been if it hadn't been Marigold.

"Yes. She's so lucky! Look." Frizz yanked open a drawer and pulled something out. "Do you like my new knickers?"

My eyes goggled. She was waving a pair of black silk knickers at me. They had a blue frilly waistband and blue frills round the legs.

"I've got another pair," said Frizz. "See?" She hoicked up her skirt. "Green ones! I didn't want pink," she said, "'cos of Keri saying pink knickers aren't cool."

"That was ages ago," I said, weakly. "That was back in Juniors. Where did you get them from?"

"Went shopping with Mum…day I went to the dentist. Got this, as well!"

Now my eyes not only goggled but started to spin like Catherine Wheels. What she was waving at me was…a bra!

"What d'you want that for?" I said.

Frizz giggled again. "What d'you think? To keep my boobs in!"

It was true that she did have boobs; of a sort. I didn't! I'm like Mum, who was flat as a pancake all the time she was at school. I didn't want them, anyway. Stupid things! I hated them. All wobbling about. I'd thought Frizz did, too. She'd always said that she did. All last term she'd gone round hunching her shoulders, trying to pretend they weren't there. Her boobs, that is; not her shoulders. Now here she was, flaunting them. Like it was something to be proud of!

"Mum said it was time," said Frizz. And then she had the nerve to add, in these very patronising tones, "I expect you'll need one quite soon."

"No way!" I said.

"Don't you want to?" said Frizz.

"No, thank you," I said. "I'm quite happy as I am." She gave me this odd, pitying look and smiled.

"I expect you'll change your mind. D'you want to go swimming one day?"

"Could, if you like."

I was surprised she'd suggested it 'cos Frizz wasn't awfully good at swimming. Up until a short while ago she hadn't been able to swim at all. Keri had been teaching her, in her indoor pool, but she could still only do a sort of sideways crabstroke, keeping one foot on the bottom. I reckoned she just wanted to show off her new boobs. (Which did look bigger than they had a month ago. Could boobs really grow that fast??? It was a frightening thought.)

Anyway, we agreed to meet at the baths at eleven o'clock on Thursday, and I went home with Dad in the car feeling that just everything and everyone was changing far quicker than I could cope with. It was like they were all on a merry-go-round, frantically whizzing past, while I stood still and watched and got dizzy. It was very confusing.

I was even more confused on Thursday, at the swimming baths. All of a sudden, Frizz could swim! She could do a real proper breaststroke – and not keeping one foot on the bottom, either. Who could have been teaching her? I didn't remember Marigold being much of a swimmer.

I put the question to her, but she just giggled and said, "I've been practising!"

"Where?" I said. "At Cooden Beach?"

But Frizz was already ploughing off up the baths, going too fast for me to catch her.

It was ten-to-fourteens morning, which meant there were loads of kids there. Including, of course, boys. Who as usual were doing a lot of racing up and down and splashing, and shoving people in, and leaping into the water with great whoops and yells. I did my best to take no notice, though it was not easy when they came barging past and nearly drowned you.

"Don't look now," said Frizz, as we took a breather at the edge of the pool, "but there's a boy over there that keeps staring at you."

"Where?" I spun my head round, indignantly.

"I said don't look!" squealed Frizz. "That one over there in the black trunks."

She was right. What cheek! He wasn't just staring, he was actually baring his teeth.

"He's smiling at you!" said Frizz. "Who is he?"

I said, "I don't know."

"He's cute!"

"Stop looking at him!"

"All right," said Frizz, "but he's still smiling. I think he fancies you!"

I was so cross ('cos it was really embarrassing) that I shot back into the water and went swimming off up the pool as fast as I could go. Frizz flopped in after me and came huffing and puffing in my wake. When we reached the far end and turned, the boy in the black trunks had disappeared. Well, I thought he had. To my intense annoyance, as we were slowly swimming our way back, he passed us, going in the opposite direction. He was grinning like an idiot. At me! I felt like saying, in tones of extreme haughtiness, "Do I know you?" But then he might have said yes and then I would have felt stupid. 'Cos it is a fact that when I am not wearing my glasses I am somewhat short-sighted. Well, very short-sighted, actually. Even when I am wearing them I have been known to walk past people without recognising them, though personally I think that is more likely to be because I am busy inventing things in my head. Poems, and stories, and things. It can make you a bit vague.

In any case, I cannot talk and swim at the same time. Some people can; but I can't. It makes me swallow oceans of water and start choking.

Frizz is obviously one of those people that can. As soon as we were out of earshot she paddled alongside of me and hissed, "That was him!"

She kept on and on about it. It really seemed to excite her. I did so hope she wasn't going to go the same way as Chloë!

Chapter 4

There were still two weeks of the summer holidays to go. These are some of the entries I made in my diary:

Took Bundle for a walk.
Took Bundle for a walk.
Bundle met his girlfriend.
Rained all morning.
Still raining. Quarrelled with Craig.
Went shopping with Mum. Got some new shoes for school. Boring ones, with laces. Mum said, "Going to school is not a

fashion statement."
Took Bundle for a walk. He rolled in fox poo.
Quarrelled with Craig. He is impossible.
I HATE BOYS.
Back to school next week. Hooray!

From which you will deduce (a good word!) that my life was not exactly what my foul and disgusting brother would call "a bundle of laughs". Just nothing happened! I had never known so much not happen before. I couldn't believe that I was back to writing in my diary! Only last term I'd been so busy that I'd had to give up. Now here I was, making all these boring entries about absolutely nothing. Taking Bundle for walks was my main activity, and losing my glasses was like a Big Event. Buying a new pair of shoes was just so-o-o exciting I could hardly stand it! Especially brown ones. Frizz went out and bought bras and frilly knickers: I went out and bought brown shoes. With laces. Big deal!

Not that I would have wanted a bra or frilly knickers. I am not a frilly knicker sort of person (I wouldn't have thought Frizz was, either) and I didn't have any boobs so a bra would have been no use to me. But I did see some brilliant new trainers! They were called "trainer skates" and they had pop-up wheels underneath, and I would have just died for a pair. They only cost £80, and as I pointed out to Mum it would save me wearing out my shoes as I would be able to skate everywhere. Mum, however, said that I had already had a little spending spree before going on holiday, and reminded me that she and Dad had also had to pay for my time at camp. "Which did not come cheap!"

It was very hard to think that I had spent all that long time being utterly miserable when I could not only have been with Frizz, enjoying myself, but could also have had my trainer skates. At least then I would have had a form of transport; sort of. Craig had his bike, but I didn't have anything. Mum said I was too young to cycle in traffic. Being nearly two years older, and a boy, Craig is allowed to do all kinds of things that I am not. It is so unfair!

I can't remember what he and I quarrelled about, but most probably he was annoying me. On purpose. Calling me Poll Doll and tweaking my hair, or else referring to me as Pancake. Mum had told me that when she was at school that had been her nickname (on account of, like me, having no boobs) and I had stupidly told Craig, so now he'd started using it. On me! I couldn't think of anything clever to call him in return. I couldn't very well call him Goggle Eyes, when we both of us wore glasses. And his feet weren't specially big, or specially splatty, and his teeth didn't stick out. Unfortunately! On the other hand his voice was starting to do that thing that boys' voices do; it was going all funny and foghorny. He kept honking like a frog. So for a bit I called him Froggy or Hooter Voice until Mum heard me and told me sharply "not to make fun of your brother". To which I heatedly retorted that in that case he shouldn't make fun of me.

"How do you mean?" said Mum.

I said, "Calling me Pancake."

"Craig?" She looked at him, reproachfully. "I hope that's not true?"

Craig got a bit sullen at this and muttered that "It was only what you used to be called".

"Yes, but not by my brother," said Mum. And she told us that it was high time we started to grow up and learn a bit of respect for each other.

So after that we only hurled insults in private. Mum is actually quite nice, but she can get really snakey if you cross her. Craig would go, "Howdy doody, Pancake!" when he knew that Mum was out of earshot. I would hiss "Hooter Voice!" when we bumped into each other on the stairs.

Of course, we didn't quarrel all the time. Just quite a lot of it! It was probably because it was the end of the holidays and we had nothing much else to do.

"Why don't you ring Dawn?" said Mum, one day. "Instead of mooning about like a lost soul."

I said, "I feel like a lost soul...I could be skating round on my trainer skates! I could be saving shoe leather! I could be—"

"You could be ringing Dawn," said Mum.

I said, "I already have. She wasn't there."

I'd rung Frizz twice. Both times her mum had answered the phone and said, "Oh, Polly! I'm so sorry. Dawn's not here at the moment. I'll get her to call you."

But that had been yesterday, and she still hadn't called. I wasn't going to try again! To try again would be like begging, almost. I shouldn't have to beg! Frizz was my best friend. Where was she? What was she doing? Why wasn't she ringing me?

In the end I couldn't bear it, so I gave in and picked up the phone and tried yet again. I got her dad this time. He said, "Hello, young Poll! If it's our Dawn you want, I'm afraid you're out of luck... She's off on some cookery thing."

Well. At least that explained it. A cookery thing. She wouldn't have invited me along to a cookery thing. I am not into cooking; Mum says she despairs. She says, "What will you do when you're on your own? You can't spend your whole life eating junk food!"

She doesn't say this to Craig, because he is a boy. Boys are allowed to eat junk food. Either that, or they have girlfriends who cook for them. So sexist! Though actually, to be fair, Craig does know how to boil an egg. And he once cooked dinner and most of it was eatable. Which it wouldn't have been if I'd done it.

On the whole I didn't feel so bad once I knew that Frizz was at a cookery thing, though I did think she might have told me. Her dad said that this time he would definitely get her to ring me. "As soon as she comes in! I shall rap her knuckles."

I said that there wasn't any actual hurry. I didn't want him to think that Frizz was the only friend I had, or that I was desperate or anything. But her dad said, "No, she deserves it! You can't ignore old friends like that. Very bad manners!" So then I felt about this size. Like he was thinking, "Poor Polly! She has no one else to hang out with."

It didn't help that it was true. Just at that moment

I didn't have anybody else to hang out with. Keri was still away. I'd tried ringing Chloë but there wasn't ever any reply, so I thought she'd probably gone off somewhere with her mum and dad; and anyway, I was still a bit miffed with her because of the way she'd behaved. Deserting me for a boy. Lastly of all, I rang Lily.

The only reason I left it till last was 'cos I knew Lily would want to tell me all about her holiday and how brilliant it had been, and then I would have to tell her that mine had been brilliant, too (because of pride, etc.) when what I really felt like doing was pouring out my thoughts about boys. The way Frizz had responded hadn't been at all satisfactory. I wanted someone to agree with me! I wanted someone to say what a nuisance they were, and what a drag, and how they ruined everything. I wasn't sure that Lily was the right person. She had boys at her dancing school and seemed to think there was nothing the matter with them. Perhaps boys that did dancing were more sensitive than boys like Craig, or the ones at camp.

Anyway, I needn't have bothered leaving Lily till last, and making up things that I could tell her about my holiday, because as it happened she wasn't there. Her mum said she'd gone to stay with a friend from dancing school. Keri was away, Chloë was away, Lily was away…everyone was away except me and Frizz. And Frizz never bothered to ring!

Her dad must have done what he said and rapped her knuckles 'cos later that day I got a phone call from her. Hugely apologetic.

"Pollee! I'm sorry I didn't ring sooner, I've been at this cookery thing."

"Yes," I said, "your dad told me."

"I only discovered about it last week; I didn't think there'd be any places left. I'd have asked you," said Frizz, "but I thought you wouldn't be interested." She giggled. "I still remember your mum telling me about the time you tried to make a cake!"

"Oh, yes. Ha ha," I said.

My cake hadn't just sagged in the middle, it had gone hard, like a concrete block. Craig had attacked it with a hammer and a chunk had gone flying across the room and cracked a glass. Ho ho! Very funny. (I don't think, actually, that a mother ought to tell these sorts of things to people. I think they should be kept secret, within the family. Otherwise it is too shameful and you are never allowed to forget it.)

"Would you have wanted to come?" said Frizz, obviously a bit alarmed by my silence.

"Me?" I said. "No way!"

"I didn't think you would." She sounded relieved.

I said, "So is it finished now?"

"Yes! Worse luck. I really enjoyed it! I learnt ever such a lot. I wish it could have gone on for ever! It's what I'm going to do when I leave school. I've decided, definitely."

Frizz is so lucky! I haven't the least idea what I am going to do when I leave school. I wish I had! I think it would be good to have something to aim for.

"So shall we see each other?" said Frizz. "We ought to see each other before we go back! Shall I come round? I could come tomorrow. If that's all right," she said. "Do you want to look in your diary?"

"Um…no. Tomorrow should be OK," I said. "I don't think I have any other engagements."

I then had the distinct suspicion that Frizz giggled. What was there to giggle about? People do have engagements. That is the whole point of keeping a diary: to remind yourself what you are doing and when you are doing it.

I put the phone down and reflected that being a celeb had done things to Frizz. We were still best friends, but it seemed that we were friends in a different kind of way. If anyone had ever had to say sorry before, it had always been me. Sorry I couldn't meet, or sorry I hadn't rung, or sorry I'd muddled my engagements. Now it was Frizz saying sorry to me! I wasn't sure that I liked it. And since when had she gone off doing her own thing without me?

I remembered how ages ago, before we left Juniors, Mum had warned me that as we grew up, the four of us, we would start to move apart. She'd said, "You'll make new friends, you'll develop new interests." I hadn't believed her at the time. Now I thought perhaps she might be right. It was horrible! If this was growing up, then I didn't want to do it! Why couldn't things stay nice and cosy, the way they had always been?

When Frizz came next day I was up in my room, sitting at my workstation. (I didn't want her to think that I was just pathetically waiting, with nothing else to do.) I heard Mum open the door and say, "Dawn! How nice to see you. You're looking very well." Then she called up the stairs, "Pollee! Dawn's here."

I went and peered over the banisters. "Oh, hi," I said. "I'll just come down."

I switched off the computer and tidied my desk, then slowly went down to the hall. Frizz was in the kitchen, talking to Mum in a very grown-up fashion about food. She seemed to be telling her how to mix milk and something or other without it curdling. Mum was saying, "Ah! Right. I'll try that."

Honestly! Frizz – telling Mum. And Mum taking it dead seriously!

"Let's go into the garden," I said. But lo and behold, what was out there but a horde of boys. Craig and his friend Jobsy and some other boy, messing with their bikes. They all looked up as Frizz and I appeared.

Craig said, "Poll Doll! And the Frizzle."

At least he didn't call me Pancake. (He probably knew, if he did, I'd call him Hooter Voice.) Jobsy and the other boy just gawped, which is what boys quite often do.

"What are you up to?" I said.

"What's it look like?"

"Looks like you're turning the garden into a tip," I said.

Craig did his honking laugh and a gobbet of spit landed on my glasses. I shrieked and said, "You pig!" And then I took my glasses off to clean them and the boy that wasn't Jobsy, that I didn't think I'd ever seen before, took on the same fuzzy shape as the boy at the baths. I put my glasses back on and looked at him, and he was the boy at the baths. All brightly pink with the same soppy smirk on his face. I recognised him, now, as a friend of Craig's. That explained why he had been grinning at me. But why couldn't he just have introduced himself, like any normal person?

I grumbled to Frizz about it as we made our way back upstairs. (We didn't want to stay in the garden with boys.) "I mean, why didn't he just say hello, like any normal person?"

"Maybe he's shy," said Frizz. "Or maybe he thought it was you but wasn't quite sure. Look! I've brought my holiday snaps to show you."

I hadn't taken any holiday snaps, but I made lots of ooh and aah noises as Frizz showed me hers, 'cos that's what you have to do when people show you photographs. One was of her and Marigold and a couple of…boys. I said, "Who are they???"

Frizz turned faintly plum-coloured. "Oh, just some guys we met on the beach. That one –" she pointed – "was called Noel, and that one was Justin. They sort of…hung around. We didn't party or anything. But they were OK. As guys go."

I said, "Hm!" Personally I was more interested in the tail end of a dog that had got into the picture. "Nice pooch," I said.

Frizz hadn't even noticed! And it was really cute.

After we'd looked at her photos she said could we go up the road to the shops. She wanted to see if she could find a copy of this teen mag called *GirlTime* that Marigold had said she'd simply got to buy.

We went back out into the garden so that we could use the side gate and avoid having to walk half way round the block. Craig and his friends were still busy working on their bikes. The grinning one, whose name I had just remembered was Nicholas Marks, tried to open the gate for us and somehow managed to get his finger caught in the bolt. We stood waiting, while he struggled to get it out again. He kept going "Oops!" and grinning, and jiggling up and down. In the end, Craig had to come and rescue him.

"Poor boy," said Frizz, as we set off for the shops.

"I think he must be a bit simple," I said. I mean, really! How on earth do you get a finger stuck in a bolt?

"He fancies you," said Frizz.

I told her witheringly not to be so ridiculous. I didn't want some idiot boy fancying me! In any case, how would that make him get his finger stuck?

"It could," said Frizz. "It's the sort of thing that happens when you're embarrassed."

I said, "Why should he be embarrassed?"

"Well, if he fancies you. Like there you were," said

Frizz, "almost within touching distance…" And she stretched out a hand and wiggled her fingers at me.

"Oh, look, just stop it!" I said. I gave her a shove. "This is boring!" It was boring and it was stupid and I didn't want to know. "Let's go and get this magazine that you want."

When we got back, Craig and his mates were just leaving. Craig had already pushed his bike out of the gate, with Jobsy pushing after him, followed by the other one. Nicholas. His face as he saw us went bright scarlet. He practically crushed himself into the gatepost in his efforts not to come too close.

"See?" I said to Frizz, as they cycled off. "He doesn't want to touch me."

"You reckon?" said Frizz, giving me this sly look.

"Yes," I said, "I do, so just shut up!"

It was all NONSENSE.

And then Frizz's mum came to pick her up and Craig arrived back home as I was saying goodbye to her. The boy was with him. For a horrible moment I thought he was going to come in, but at the last minute, to my relief, he peeled off and went cycling on up the road.

"That was Knickers," said Craig, wheeling his bike through the gate. "He's got this thing about you…"

Chapter 5

I said, "What do you mean, *thing*? What *thing*? What are you talking about?"

"Knickers," said Craig. "He fancies you like crazy!"

I felt my cheeks go roaring into the red zone. I do so hate it when people make me blush!

I said crossly, "I think you must be mad."

Craig honked. "He's the one that's mad…fancying an old bag like you!"

I said, "Just shut up, Hooter Voice!"

"Pancake!"

"Frog."

"Way to go!" cried Craig, leaping up and punching the air.

Don't ask me what it's supposed to mean. Craig talks a language of his own. He picks it up off the telly, from movies that he shouldn't be watching, and thinks it's cool. Well, it isn't! It's just stupid.

"I've told him you're a man-hater," said Craig.

"I am not!" I shrieked.

"You are, you're a man-hater!"

"*Boy* hater," I said.

"Same thing!"

"'S not! Men are OK. Boys are just...*yuck*."

"So are girls, when they're like you. Fortunately," said Craig, "not all of them are. Only the old bags!"

I expect we might have gone on like this indefinitely if Mum hadn't suddenly appeared and said, "Craig and Polly, if you've nothing better to do than shout abuse at each other perhaps you'd like to go and clean up the front garden for me... Here!" And she handed me a pair of rubber gloves and thrust a green plastic sack at Craig. "Make a good job of it, please! Your gran's coming tomorrow, I don't want the place looking like a tip."

Resentfully, we trundled round the front with our gloves and our sack. The front garden was A MESS.

Local litter louts had chucked beer cans over the fence and parked empty bottles in the hedge and dumped the remains of their Kentucky frieds in the flower beds. There were also sweet wrappers, cigarette packets, travel cards, phone cards, bus passes, and general assorted rubbish. Rubbish is the bane of Mum's life! It is such a shame 'cos she loves her garden and really likes to see it look nice.

"You pick, I'll stash," said Craig.

"Why do I always get the worst job?" I said, clawing up a pile of chicken bones.

"'Cos you're smaller than me...you can get under things easier."

I said, "Hmph!" And then, "Oh, look! There's a letter." I sat back on my heels to see what it said.

"Stop reading other people's mail!" roared Craig.

"I can read it if I want," I said. "It's in our garden."

"It's a criminal offence, that is," said Craig. "Opening other people's mail."

"It was already open. Anyway, it's boring," I said, stuffing it in the sack. "It's just about someone not paying their gas bill, so they're the criminal, not me. So there! Ugh, this is loathsome."

"I told him you were a man-hater," said Craig. "And you're a pancake! I don't know what he sees in you."

71

"Well, I certainly don't see anything in him," I said, turning tomato all over again. "I hope he's not going to keep coming round and ogling."

"Do what?" said Craig. He's not a word person any more than Frizz or Lily.

"Ogling," I said. And I put on this silly smirk and swivelled my eyes about.

"Oh, you mean like perving," said Craig. "You should be so lucky! You've missed a load of stuff over by the fence."

"You get it!"

"You've got the gloves, it's your job. I'm the sack man. You fetch, I carry. He wants to know if you'll go out with him."

"What?" I jerked upright at great speed and bashed my head against the side of the house. "Ow! No! Course I won't go out with him!"

"Why not?"

"'Cos I don't want to!"

"'Cos you're a man-hater!"

"'Cos I don't know him!" I screamed.

"He doesn't know you," said Craig. "If he did, he'd run a mile. Anyone would! Just to get away from you. Flat old bag!"

"Shut up," I said. "I've hurt myself."

"Serve you right. You'll end up on the shelf, you will."

I said, "What shelf?"

"Shelf full of old wrinkled bags that nobody wants!"

I shrieked, "Yes, and you'll end up on another one full of sexist pigs!"

"That's right," said Craig, "have a go at pigs."

I fell silent when he said that 'cos I always think it's so unfair when people talk of sexist pigs or spiteful cats, or say, for instance, that football hooligans are like animals. I once made a vow not to do it, but I keep forgetting.

Craig threw his plastic sack over his shoulder and I took off Mum's rubber gloves, which were far too big for me, and we set off back round the corner.

"Look!" I said. I giggled. "You can make these go like balloons!"

I blew into a glove until it was all fat and pouchy, then pinched the ends together and squeeeeeezed until a big transparent bubble appeared. I then started blobbing Craig about the head with it, dancing on and off the kerb as I batted at him.

"Watch out!" yelled Craig. He grabbed my arm and yanked me back on to the pavement as a car shot past. "You stupid daft cow, you could have got run over!"

I said, "Don't call me that. Cows aren't stupid."

"No? Well, you are!" He bashed me with his sack. "How'd you think I'd have felt if you'd gone and got yourself squashed?"

"Shouldn't think you'd care," I muttered, though I was feeling a bit shaken, to tell the truth. I am always doing these really silly things. "Shouldn't think it'd matter to you one way or the other."

"Have you made a will?" said Craig.

I said, "No! And I wouldn't leave you anything even if I had."

"It's just that I'd like your computer."

"What for?" I said. "You've already got one."

"Yeah, well, I'd like two... You leave me your computer, and I'll leave you my bike. Deal?"

"I'll think about it," I said, pushing my way in through the back gate.

"What about Knickers? What shall I tell him?"

"Tell him what you like," I said.

There was half an hour to go before tea. I went upstairs to my room and studied myself in the long mirror that is on the inside of my wardrobe door. I was wearing a pink top with a big blue butterfly printed on it, pink check trousers ("gingham", Mum said they were) and a pair of sandals. I looked about eight years old. I mean, whoever wore sandals? Especially ordinary boring ones. Keri would sooner die! And what on earth had made me get a top with a big blue butterfly on it? And trousers of pink check! I knew Keri's feelings about pink. Pink was definitely not cool.

This was terrible! I had no dress sense at all. I'd always thought it was Frizz who lacked dress sense, but when Frizz had come round she'd been wearing a really groovy pair of jeans, black ones, cropped, and combat shoes. And her top had been plain white with a sequin army patch on it. Truly cool! How come Frizz had suddenly become Miss Fashion? How come I had fallen so far behind???

I hated every single thing I was wearing. I decided that as soon as tea was over I would take Bundle up the park and trash everything. Tear it to pieces! Cover it in mud! Mum wouldn't be very pleased with me, but it was the only way. I could go on my knees and beg and she still wouldn't understand the need for new clothes while I still had the old ones.

"But, Polly," she'd go, "you've only had them a

few months! What's wrong with them?"

If I tried to explain how they made me look eight years old she'd start off on one of her "I don't want you behaving like Keri" speeches. It's not that she doesn't like Keri, just that she thinks she's a bit too cool, a bit too fashion-conscious.

"You're twelve years old, for goodness' sake! I don't want you going round all tarted up like Keri."

But twelve was almost teenage. You just don't wear blue butterflies and pink trousers when you're twelve. I'd still only been eleven and a half when I chose them. I'd done a lot of growing up since then. But it was no use saying that to Mum. She'd only tell me that when she was my age, "We wore what we were told to wear. We didn't have designer clothes!"

Over tea, Craig told Mum how I'd nearly got run over. "She's not safe! She shouldn't be allowed out."

I kicked at him under the table. He immediately kicked me back. I said, "Ouch!"

"Craig, stop that," said Mum.

"She did it first," said Craig.

"Yes," I said, "'cos you were telling tales."

"Wasn't!"

"You were!"

"Wasn't. I just wanted Mum to know," said Craig,

all full of smugness and virtue, "that you need road training."

"Yes," I screeched, "like you need potty training!"

Mum picked up the lid of the biscuit tin and banged with it on the table.

"I shall go mad," she said. "I shall go stark mad! If I had the money, I swear I'd send both of you away to boarding school!"

"Be nice," muttered Craig. "Get away from her."

Silently I mouthed at him across the table: "Froggie!"

Craig mouthed back at me: "Pancake!"

"Right," said Mum. "That's it! I've had enough. Just go away, the pair of you! Get out of my sight! Go and pick your noses or eat your toenails. Do something!"

"Mum," I said. I looked at her, reproachfully. "That is disgusting!"

"Out!" Mum hammered on the table with the handle of her knife. "Out, out, out! The pair of you!"

Craig snatched a handful of biscuits and ran for the hall. I picked up Bundle's lead and fled, with Bundle, through the back door.

"If you're taking that dog out," bawled Mum, "just watch how you go!"

I wonder if other people's mums behave like this? There really is no call for it.

Bundle and I walked up to the park. It is only a titchy little place, but it means he can meet other dogs and have a bit of a natter.

I couldn't help noticing that there were girls all over, all looking as cool as can be in trainers and tank tops and bum-hugging jeans that would have made Mum purse her lips and say, "Twelve-going-on-twenty." I was filled with envy. I wanted to be twelve-going-on-twenty!

I took Bundle past the little woody bit that he loves, as it is full of fox and badger smells. It is not a proper wood, just a few trees and some brambly mounds, but I thought maybe I could manage to tear holes in my horrible pink trousers and butterfly top.

Unfortunately it is right next to the children's playground where all these little kids were swarming up the climbing frame and jigging up and down on the seesaw, watched by their beaming mums, some of whom I recognised as they lived in our road. They were mums that knew my beaming mum, who wouldn't be very beaming if one of them happened to mention that "I saw Polly ripping her trousers to pieces in the park". So that wasn't any good.

I turned glumly to go back home, thinking that I could maybe climb up the apple tree in the garden and rend myself that way. I walked across the grass towards the paddling pool, where Craig and I used to splash about when we were young. The park suddenly seemed to be full of boys. There were boys kicking footballs, boys kicking Coke cans, boys riding bicycles. You're not supposed to ride bicycles in the park. There are big notices all round that say NO CYCLING. And there they were, doing it! They'd even dragged stuff out of the woods, old branches and tree trunks and stuff, and made ramps. They were whizzing up the ramps and flying off into space, wheeee! Then bump, bang, crash back to earth.

Bundle saw them and grew excited. He went lolloping off, all wagging and happy, to join in.

I screamed, "Bundle!" as a bike landed within centimetres of him. I hurled myself across the grass, screeching and yelling. I was really scared that he was going to get knocked over.

"You're not meant to be doing that!" I yelled, as another bike came flying off a ramp. I am normally quite a meek and mild sort of person, who wouldn't say boo to an earthworm, but I was just so angry!

"There's notices!" I yelled.

That horrible boy! All he did was make a gesture – a rude gesture – and shout something unpleasant which I am sorry but I do not intend to repeat.

I put Bundle on the lead and seethed all the way home. I foamed and frothed and gnashed with my teeth. I was in the most terrific rage.

So terrific was it that when I got in and Mum said, "Ah, just in time! Keri's on the phone", I ran at the phone and grabbed it and said "Hi" in this really belligerent tone of voice.

Keri said, "Oh. Hi!" sounding slightly surprised. "I'm back!"

And then before I even had a chance to say "Did you enjoy your holiday?", which I just might have done, out of normal politeness, she got going on it anyway. She talked for five whole minutes without stopping (I timed her) and then said, "Well, but I'll tell you all about it when we meet! We must arrange a meeting. How about next Saturday? Round my place. Ask Frizz and tell me if it's OK. I'll ask Lily. We've got to get together! I've got so much to tell! How was summer camp? Did you meet anyone dishy? What did you do? I want to hear all about it! You can tell us when we meet. I got your postcard, by the way. Did you get mine? I sent two. Did you get them? Polly?

You've gone all quiet! What's the matter?"

I said, "I'm seething, if you want to know."

Keri said, "Wow! What about?"

"Boys," I said. "On bicycles. In the park."

"Uh oh!" said Keri. "This sounds serious!"

"It is," I said. "They shouldn't be there. There's notices. It's against the law!"

Keri said, "Shock horror! Tell me more!"

So I told her about the ramps and she said, "Like a cyclo-cross. Fun!"

"But they shouldn't be there. They practically ran over Bundle! I yelled at them," I said. "They didn't take any notice."

"No, well, they wouldn't," said Keri, "would they?"

Meaning what, exactly? I held the receiver away from me and glared at it. I hoped she wasn't implying that I was too childish and insignificant to have any impact.

"One of them," I said, "gave me the finger."

"Never!"

I thought, for a second, that she was genuinely shocked, until I realised that she was making fun of me, just like that beastly boy had. She wasn't shocked at all! And if I told Craig, he probably wouldn't be shocked, either. He'd probably laugh. Everybody would laugh. I was a figure of fun!

"Are you still there?" said Keri.

I said, "Yes, but I've got to go."

"Already?"

"Yes," I said, "I've got things to do. See you soon. Byee!" And I bounced the receiver back and went racing out into the garden and down to the apple tree. I didn't care if Mum did get mad, I wasn't going to wear these babyish clothes a minute longer!

Chapter 6

Gran arrived on Saturday morning. I went with Dad to pick her up from the station, as she doesn't like to drive very far these days. Me and Gran get on pretty well. I know there are some people who complain that their grans are crabby and crotchety and read them long lectures about manners and about speaking properly and having respect. My gran isn't like that. She may be seventy-three – a big age! – but she is young at heart, Mum says. And I agree with her.

Me and Gran have these long chats together. Heart-to-hearts, Gran calls them. We exchange confidences! Gran tells me what it is like to be old, and I tell her what it is like to be young. I mean, I know that she has been young, but it was a very long time ago and she has most probably forgotten some of it. Plus of course things have changed, as she is always reminding me. "We didn't have that in my day," she goes (but not being crabby or cross).

These are just some of the things that she did not have in her day:

mobile phones,

computers,

videos,

CDs.

"Oh, but we managed!" she says. "We managed!"

I told her, that weekend, that I thought I could manage without any of those things. Well, perhaps CDs I might miss, but not any of the others. "He couldn't manage," I said, pointing at Craig. "He's a technofreak."

"Yeah," said Craig, "and you're a Stone Age nerd! We'd still be living in caves if everyone was like you!"

I wouldn't actually mind living in a cave. I said this to Gran (after Craig had gone off, mouthing "Pancake" at me as he did so). Gran said, "It might be all right when you're young, but I don't think it would be much fun when you're old. I need my home comforts!" And she told me how her poor knees were playing up something rotten.

In return I told her about my experience at summer camp. How there had been boys there, and how Chloë – "Who is supposed to be my friend!" – had deserted me in favour of the Gangle.

"It's hard when that happens," said Gran. "I remember it happened to me once. My best friend, Pat Garibaldi…she was a right one for the boys! They clustered round that girl like flies round a honey pot." She laughed, and shook her head. "I was always the odd one out. The wallflower. Wilting in the corner, all by myself. But then I grew up and met your granddad and got married and had your mum and your Uncle Clive, and what happened to Pat Garibaldi?"

"What?" I said, hoping that it might be something really bad.

"Didn't settle down till she was nearly forty. Having too much fun! Used to laugh at me, she did. Stuck at home with a couple of kids… You're missing out, she used to say. Then in the end she found she'd left it too late. They tried for a baby, but it was no go. She never managed it. It's a terrible thing," said Gran, "when you can't have children."

I looked at her, doubtfully. It didn't seem so very terrible to me.

"Would you have liked it," I said, "if boys had clustered round you like flies round a honey pot instead of round Pat Garibaldi?"

"Well, probably not just at first," admitted Gran. "I think I'd have been embarrassed. I was a bit of a slow starter, to tell you the truth." She leaned towards me. "Don't tell your mum," she whispered, "but I was still playing with my dolls when I was your age."

I said, "Gran!" I had given up playing with dolls years ago.

"True as I sit here," said Gran. "While Pat Garibaldi was painting her lips with her mum's lipstick, I was teaching the alphabet to a load of dolls."

I giggled.

"All I'm saying is," said Gran, "it's nothing to be ashamed of. Some of us mature fast, some of us mature more slowly. You can't rush these things. It may seem like your friend Chloë's galloping away from you right now, but you'll catch up with her. Just give it time."

I knew Gran was trying to make me feel better, but I wasn't sure that I wanted to catch up. Not if it meant mooning around after boys, going all goggle-eyed and gooey. Gran must have read my thoughts, or maybe I had this look on my face that said "No way!" She leaned forward and patted my knee as I sat cross-legged in front of her. "You'll see! It'll happen. It's a bit like learning to drive. You think, 'I'm never going to go on the motorway!' And then one day you just find yourself on it and it seems the most natural thing in the world."

"Not to me," I said. "I'm not ever going to drive. I hate cars! They pollute the atmosphere. They're ruining the planet!"

"A bit like boys, eh?"

"Exactly!" I said.

Gran smiled. "You'll find when you get to know them that they're not so bad."

Not so bad???

"Just look at Craig!" I said.

"Ah, that's different," said Gran. "He's your brother."

"But he calls me Pancake!"

"And what do you call him?"

"Well…" Another fit of giggles came over me. "I call him Hooter Voice. But he deserves it! He started it!"

"Oh, you will look back on all this and have a good laugh together one of these days," said Gran. "You mark my words! When you're both grown up, with children of your own—"

"It's all right when they're grown up," I said. "It's when they're boys they're so horrid!"

"I'll tell you what," said Gran. "I bet you anything you like that by this time next year you'll be singing a different tune!"

If she meant I would have changed my mind then she was wrong.

"Bet I won't!" I said.

Gran leapt in, sharp as could be. She's still ever so much on the ball. Dad says she doesn't miss a trick.

"How much?" she said. "How much do you bet?"

I said, "I'll bet you…" And then I stopped, because I didn't want to bet money. I mean, just suppose – horror of horrors! – that Gran turned out to be right??? She wouldn't. But just suppose…

"I'll bet you a five pound book token," said Gran, "against a week's worth of telephone calls… If you lose, you promise to ring me up every night for a week! How about that?"

"All right," I said. "And you'll give me a book token?"

"Only if I lose," said Gran. "But I can tell you right here and now…I won't!"

I thought, poor Gran, she simply has no idea. But I

did look forward to getting my book token!

On Monday we went back to school. I'd been looking forward to the start of the new term. For lots of reasons. To begin with, I was now in Year Eight. I could hardly believe it! A year ago I had been a creepy crawly new girl not knowing a soul (apart from Jessamy Jones, who came from Juniors. But Jessamy Jones is not the sort of person that you would want to know.) Now I had a whole bunch of friends. Katie and Chantal and Beverley, and of course Chloë, who was my best one. I knew my way around, I knew all the rules, I knew most of the teachers, which ones were nice, which ones were nasty, which ones could be really mean. Best of all, I could look at the new kids and feel superior!

Another reason I'd been looking forward to going back was that at last, I thought, life could return to normal. Normal being loads of homework (which I don't really mind), lots of cosy gossip in the playground at break, lots of giggling and chattering and exchanging notes with Chloë. Plus Saturday meetings with the Gang, which I'd really missed during the long summer holidays. We had never been apart for so long! And I had never, ever seen so little of Frizz.

To begin with, that first day, everything seemed just

the way it ought to be. Chantal had got there first and saved seats for the rest of us – Katie, Chloë, me, Bev – all along the back row, which is where we like to be. (Not so that we can mess around but because, as Chantal says, it is a more commanding position.)

Mr Singh was our class teacher, and that was OK, even though he is Geography and Geography happens to be a subject I am totally useless at. Mr Singh forgives me even when I muddle up Madrid and Madras! He is not like Mrs Mountjoy, who shouts at people. Mrs Mountjoy teaches Science, which is another subject I am useless at. I had been dreading in case we had her! So when the door opened and Mr Singh walked in, it was a great weight off my shoulders. I thought, "I am really going to enjoy this term!"

We blocked in our timetables, and there was double Maths on Monday (ugh, yuck, bummer, as Craig would say), but double French on Tuesdays (hooray! I like French) and Latin on Wednesdays and Fridays, with Drama all of Wednesday afternoon and lots and lots of English, which is my best subject of all.

At first break we went out into the playground, which needless to say nobody actually plays in. Not even the kids in Year Seven, though sometimes they do tend to racket about a bit, still being rather young.

But mostly, on the whole, we just stroll around or sit and talk. The sixth form have their own garden, but the rest of us are all herded together.

Eagerly, as we headed for our favourite seat before anyone else could bag it, I said to Chloë, "I am just so relieved we haven't got Mrs Mountjoy!"

Chloë said, "Yeah, me, too. Hey, Chantal!" She waved across the playground. "Over here!"

Chantal and Katie came running over, to be joined almost immediately by Bev – and then, the cheek of it, by Ms J. Jones. What nerve! She wasn't one of us! What right did she think she had to come barging in where she wasn't wanted? Nobody told her to go away – I suppose it would have seemed a bit rude, even though she herself was being rude as could be, I mean pushing in like that – so she stayed where she was, cramming her body between Chantal and Katie and shouting her way, totally uninvited, into the conversation.

Chloë had started talking about holidays, which I'd been secretly hoping she wouldn't, but everyone always wants to say where they've gone. Bev had gone on a camping trip round France with her mum and dad. Chantal had gone to Disneyworld (in Florida!). Katie had stayed with her mum's family in Ireland. Jessamy Jones boasted, in her loud clanging voice, that she had gone to Gran Canaria. She gets right up my nose, that girl!

Chloë, of course, went and told everyone how we had been to summer camp.

Jessamy said, "Ooooh! Were there any boys?"

Chloë giggled and said, "Loads!"

"Was there anyone you fancied?"

Chloë did the thing with her eyes, making them go all big. "And how!"

"Tell, tell!" screeched Jessamy.

"He's called Rob, and he's gorgeous! Isn't he?" Chloë turned to me. "Didn't you think he was gorgeous?"

I nearly said, "He had red hair", but I stopped myself just in time. Katie has red hair! In any case, you oughtn't to pick on people's physical characteristics. The Gangle couldn't help having red hair any more than I can help having to wear glasses. So I hunched a shoulder and said, "If you like that kind of thing."

Chloë went bright scarlet. Jessamy said, "Well, get her!" Meaning me. All the others pulled these reproachful-type faces like I'd said something really mean, which I suppose perhaps I had, but they hadn't had to put up with four whole weeks of Chloë mooning about like a lovesick hen.

"I'm sure he was absolutely fabbo," said Jessamy.

Chantal wanted to know if Chloë was going to keep in touch with him. Her face lit up (it had fallen a bit after my bad-tempered outburst, which to be honest I was already regretting). She said, "Yes! We email like crazy and send text messages all the time. At half term we're going to try and meet up."

"Oh! Oh!" cried Jessamy. "It's the real thing!"

Chloë turned pink – but this time it was with pleasure. I mean, you could tell.

"She's in lurv!" Jessamy clasped both hands to her bosom (which was just about becoming noticeable). "The first one of us!"

I found it so weird. It's not even as if Chloë is pretty. Not like Chantal, for instance. Chantal is black and sleek, like a panther, and just so beautiful it almost hurts. But she wasn't in love! She didn't even seem to have a boyfriend. How come Chloë had got one? Even if it was only the Gangle. Chloë is my friend and she is very bright and very funny, but her teeth stick out and her hair is all mad and messy and she would be the first to admit that she would not win any beauty contests. Yet she had got there before any of us! It was a great mystery, and also quite upsetting. To me, at any rate.

The others didn't seem to think it in the least bit

strange. They took it all dead seriously and kept asking these dumb yucky questions such as, "Did he kiss you?" and "What was it like?" and "Did he use his tongue?" (*Yeeeeurgh!*)

They couldn't get enough. Especially Jessamy. As the bell rang for the end of break and we moved off across the playground, she seized Chloë by the arm and gushily started telling her about this guy she had met in Gran Canaria.

"He wanted to kiss me, but I wouldn't let him 'cos I mean he must have been at least twenty. I think twenty's way too old, don't you?"

Chloë nodded and said, "Yes. Definitely!" All of a sudden, there was this bond between them. The bond of boys. And I was being left out all over again! I mooched miserably behind them into school. Only last term Chloë had grumbled to me about Jessamy Jones being so bossy and pushy and altogether unbearable. Now they were, like, all matey-matey and bosom pals.

"It's my birthday next month," said Jessamy. "I'm going to have a big party. And I'm going to invite simply oodles of boys!"

Chloë screamed. Katie screeched. Chantal went into a pretend swoon. Bev, breathless, said, "Where are you going to get them from?"

"Anywhere! Everywhere! Just leave it to me!"

"Are *we* invited?" said Chantal.

"All of you! But just you lot. Don't go round blabbing about it to anyone else, 'cos I don't want any of the others. Just you guys, 'cos you're my friends!"

I thought, "Since when?" and spent the rest of the day wondering what excuse I could make not to go. I still remembered the last time I had been to a party with boys. Everyone had gone all silly and ganged up against me, making me dance with this poor little guy called Jack that was only about nine years old, pretending that he was my boyfriend. It had just been so embarrassing. For both of us. I didn't want to go through that again!

As we left school at the end of the day, Jessamy came bustling past all full of self-importance.

"The twelfth of October," she hissed. "Keep it free!"

That night I made a big entry in my diary. Under Saturday 12th October I wrote:

JESSAMY JONES'S BIRTHDAY PARTY

I did it to remind myself not to go...

Chapter 7

On Saturday we had our Gang of Four meeting round at Keri's. The first time we had got together since breaking up in July. Two whole months!

Dad had offered to take me, so we stopped off on the way for Frizz. She was wearing her cropped jeans and her top with the Army patch and a new pair of trainers. Really swanky ones with soles about 10 cm thick. Like mini Hovercrafts! I said this to her and she said, "Oh, do you think so?" But not like she terribly cared. Like, who was I to offer an opinion?

I said, "Where did you get them from?" Meaning,

actually, how could your mum and dad afford them, except you can't ask a person a thing like that. But I had never *ever* seen Frizz wearing such flash gear before.

"Got them from New Wave," she said. "Got everything from New Wave."

And then she obviously felt that some kind of an explanation was called for and added that her gran had won a thousand pounds on the Lottery and had given her some money to spend on clothes.

Gulp! I knew I oughtn't to be jealous, 'cos in the past poor old Frizz had never had money to spend on clothes, but I just couldn't help it. Mum had been cross as hornets when I'd ripped my despised butterfly top and my horrible pink trousers to pieces, climbing up the apple tree. I'd tried explaining to her that I'd gone up the tree to rescue what I'd thought was a cat, only then when I'd got there it hadn't been a cat, and on the way down I'd gone and slipped and could quite easily have killed myself, which you'd think any normal mum would be far more bothered about than just a few torn clothes, but somehow I don't think she believed me. She had that *look*. Which is this look she gets when she suspects you're not telling the exact truth. I think she may actually have thought that I'd done it on purpose. As if!

Anyway, she absolutely point blank refused to give me any money for new clothes. She said, "The summer's nearly over, it would be a total waste. You'll have grown out of them by this time next year."

I said, "But, Mum, we've got global warming! The climate is getting *hotter*."

She said, "What has that to do with it?"

"It means I'll still be needing summer clothes even in the darkest depths of winter," I told her.

"Too bad!" said Mum. "You'll just have to make do."

So now I was wearing an old yucky top that I'd once considered to be the height of style, but which was now so past its sell-by date it should have been ripped up for rags, plus a pair of jeans that I'd cropped with the garden shears. I hadn't been able to keep a straight line, which meant that they were jagged, and all where I'd hacked was hanging in shreds, which Bundle kept trying to chew.

Craig said, "Hey, do you know part of your jeans is missing?" I informed him (witheringly) that it was the fashion, and he said, "Oh, sorry! I thought the bugs must have got at them." *Idiot*.

Even Dad was stupid. As I climbed into the car he said, "Where did you get those from? The Recycling

Unit?" And he laughed, as if he'd said something really funny.

I said, "These are the only jeans I've got. They're so old they're falling to pieces, but Mum won't let me have any new ones."

I said it in the hope that Dad (who is a far softer touch than Mum) might put his hand in his pocket and pull out some notes and say, "I cannot have my only daughter going round in rags! Go and get yourself a new pair right away."

But he didn't. He just laughed again, as if this time *I* had said something funny, and told me that "In my day we used to jump in a cold bath to shrink them. Now you're chopping them to pieces! I dunno."

I said, "*Da-a-ad!*"

Dad, imitating me, said, "*Ye-e-e-es?*"

I said, "Dad, it's serious! I'll get a complex!"

"That should be interesting," said Dad.

There are times when I think that men are as bad as boys. It is always ho-ho-ho and jokey-jokey. They just never take anything seriously! Not unless it's their boring football. I mean, who cares who wins the stupid Cup? I once said this to Craig and he was, like, totally gobsmacked. He just couldn't believe I'd said it! Anyway, it shut him up.

When we got to Keri's place, Keri and Lily were already in their bathing costumes, splashing about in Keri's indoor pool. Keri's indoor pool is lovely! (It was put in by my dad.) The water is always warm. Plus of course you don't have *boys* charging up and down and nearly drowning you.

Frizz and I stripped off (we had our cozzies on underneath our clothes) and jumped in. I could see Keri's mouth falling open as Frizz struck out towards the deep end.

"Where did she learn to do that?"

"I don't know," I said.

"Wow! I'm impressed," said Keri.

"She can swim better than we can!" said Lily, meaning her and me.

"I know," I said. "It's weird!"

After we'd been in the pool a while Keri's mum and dad appeared, so we dried ourselves off and went upstairs to Keri's room to drink Coke and eat crisps and have a natter. Keri's mum and dad are quite nice, but you can't be cosy and enjoy a gossip with grown-ups about.

"So!" Keri bounced herself on to the window seat. "Holidays. Let's all tell. Lily! You start."

I'd known this would happen, so when it came to

my turn I just said that I'd gone pony trekking and hiking and orienteering and sung lots of songs round the camp fire.

"Sounds like fun," said Keri. "Did you enjoy the pony trekking?"

"No," I said. "I came off."

"Oh, you *didn't*?" said Keri. "Polly! How could you?"

"I just did," I said.

I think Lily could see that I didn't specially want to talk about it 'cos she rolled over on to her stomach and said, "So what's new? What's happening in everyone's life?"

"Yes! What are we all up to?" said Frizz.

"Back to school," I said, and gave a ritual groan, in which Frizz and Keri joined. But not Lily! Lily just adores every single moment of being at dance school. I can see that it must be bliss to spend half of every day doing something you really enjoy. She has to do ordinary stuff as well, of course; Maths and French and stuff. But not nearly as much of it, it seems to me, as the rest of us. I would like to spend my time doing French and Latin and English, with maybe just a bit of History and a bit of Art, but *nothing else*. Nothing else *whatsoever*. Especially not Maths or Science or

Geography. Or gym or hockey or being forced to run round the edge of the playing field in icy weather pursued by Miss Brewer, who is all beefy and hearty and loud. She always yells at me, "Come along, Polly Roberts! Keep up! Put some effort into it!" I would like to drop *all* of those things.

Some hope!

We talked for a bit about school, all the good things and the bad things. Keri complained that she and her friend Mima had been put in separate dorms because they were a bad influence on each other. "Just because at the end of last term we organised a midnight feast!"

"Do things like that really happen?" I said. "I thought it was just in books."

"Why should it just be in books?" said Keri.

"Did you have sardines and chocolate cake?" Frizz wanted to know. "That's what they usually have. And then they get sick and have to go to the san!"

Keri said, "We had champagne and got drunk." She giggled. "We all woke up with the most terrific hangovers. Andrea Martin couldn't even get out of bed!"

"In that case," said Lily, busy doing stretching

exercises on the floor, "I'm not surprised they've separated you."

"Why?" said Keri. "Just 'cos we had a bit of champagne?"

"Having too much to drink is bad for you," said Lily.

"Where did you get it from?" said Frizz.

"Oh!" Keri waved a hand. "Mima's dad has stacks of it... She smuggled a couple of bottles into school with her."

Solemnly Lily said, "How the other half live."

"I don't like champagne anyway," I said. "Mum got some for when I passed the scholarship. I drank it, but I didn't like it."

"No, well, you wouldn't," said Keri. "You probably still have a very unsophisticated palate. You're terribly young for your age, you know, Polly. And ooh!" she squealed, as Frizz reached across for a handful of crisps, "you're wearing a bra!"

"Yes." Frizz turned pink with a sort of pleasurable embarrassment. "Mum got it for me in the holidays."

"That makes two of us!" Self-important, Keri twanged a bra strap. And then, before anyone could stop them, they'd gone off into this shrieky giggly discussion about cup sizes. I tried to catch Lily's eye so that we could exchange faces, but Lily, as usual, was concentrating on twisting her body into impossible shapes. She was sitting on the carpet with her legs spread out and was bending forward with her head touching the floor. The conversation just flowed right over her. I sometimes think that Lily lives in a world of her own.

"This girl at school," Keri was saying, "this girl in the sixth form, Titania Bulawka, she's got massive ones. Like right out here, you know?" Keri held her hands out in front of her, making like she was holding a couple of melons. Frizz nodded, earnestly. "I reckon she must be about...46E! We call her Titty. Titty Bulawka. Short for Titania," she explained, for my benefit. Just in case I hadn't got the joke.

Frizz said, "Wow! Like a Page Three Girl."

"Gross," said Lily.

"Bliss," said Frizz.

"Could come in handy," said Keri. "Like if you wanted to bash someone!"

"Bashed with a boob!"

Keri and Frizz both went off into mad peals of giggles.

"Polly, how about you?" said Keri. "Are you... um...getting anywhere yet?"

I scowled, to cover my embarrassment.

"I think they're starting to grow," said Frizz, kindly.

"Course, that one's just a lost cause." Keri jerked a thumb over her shoulder at Lily. "She'll never have any shape at all."

Lily cackled. She didn't care! She's ever so confident, in a quiet sort of way. I wish I was. I hated the thought of having boobs and having to wear a bra, but at the same time I hated being left out. I hated being told that I was young for my age! I also hated Keri and Frizz ganging up against me. In the past it had always been me sticking up for Frizz when Keri had a go at her, which she used to do quite a lot. "Frizz," she'd go, "your *hair*! Frizz, your *clothes*! Frizz, grow *up*!"

Now, suddenly, it seemed as if Frizz had overtaken me and I was the one that had to grow up. I didn't like it!

"OK. OK!" Lily whizzed herself back into a sitting position. "That's enough about boobs. What about parties? Anyone heard of any?"

"Yes!" Keri grinned, triumphantly. "I'm having one next month. It's my birthday, right?" We all nodded. "I'm going to have a Big Bash! Dad's going to hire a hall and we're going to have a real professional DJ. You will all come, won't you? Nineteenth of October.

Make a note of it!"

We promised that we would.

"That's the week after Jessamy Jones's," I said.

Keri pulled a face. "Puke. Vomit. Don't tell me she's still around?"

"Unfortunately," I said.

Jessamy had been Keri's sworn enemy at Juniors. We all hated her.

"She's having this party," I said. "But I'm not going to go. I've been invited, but she is just so disgusting."

Everyone agreed that Jessamy Jones was totally foul.

"On the other hand," said Keri, "a party is a party... I mean, you never know who you might meet."

"At Jessamy Jones's?" said Frizz.

"Well, this is it," I said. "In any case, she's having *boys*."

There was a silence.

"Honestly," I said. "She seems to think it's normal!"

"What, boys?" said Keri.

"Yes! At a *party*! I ask you!"

They were all looking at me.

"Hm! Well. Yes!" said Keri. "It's up to you, of course...whether you go."

"To Jessamy Jones's? No way!"

"Would you go?" I said to Frizz, as we drove back later, with Dad.

"Might do," said Frizz.

"But you don't like her!"

Frizz agreed that she didn't. "But I like parties!"

She never used to like them. She used to get quite nervous and worked up, in case nobody talked to her or laughed at the way she was dressed. Frizz had definitely changed. It was all very unsettling.

"Anyway," she said, "you'll come to Keri's?"

"Oh, well, yes, of course!" I said. "That's different." For one thing, Keri was my friend; and for another, there wouldn't be any boys. Of course I would go to Keri's!

We dropped Frizz off and drove on home. While Dad put the car away, I went round to the back. I was just about to push the gate open when someone the other side yanked at it and the Knickers boy came out. We bumped slap, bang! right into each other.

We both went bright scarlet.

Chapter 8

I made this excuse not to go to Jessamy's party: I said I was going to visit my gran. Chloë wailed that it would be no fun without me, but I don't think Jessamy cared. She just said, "Oh, well, in that case I'll have to ask someone else, to make the numbers up... Who shall I ask?"

She invited a girl called Samantha that as a rule we didn't have anything to do with as a) she was in another house and b) if Keri was twelve going on eighteen then Samantha was twelve going on twenty-one. Chloë giggled and said, "She's promised to bring a *boy*!" But then she admitted that Samantha was a bit scary.

"She goes out with this guy that's at sixth form college… I mean, he's nearly seventeen! What's going to happen if she brings him with her?"

I didn't know and I didn't care. I was just glad that I wasn't going! But then all day Saturday I had to skulk about indoors, not daring to set foot outside the house, not even to take Bundle up the park, in case someone from school might see me. Mum couldn't understand it. She said, "Polly, stop being so lazy and take that dog for his walk!"

I said, "Why does it always have to be me? He's Craig's dog just as much as mine! Why can't he take him?"

"Because taking him for walks is your job!" roared Craig. "I cut the grass and clean the car, you take the dog out."

I shrieked, "Don't call him the dog! He's Bundle."

"Yes, and you're the one that takes him out!"

In the end I had to, for the sake of peace and quiet. I didn't want Mum interrogating me, and also I couldn't stand to see poor Bundle pathetically waiting by his lead. So we rushed up to the park as quick as could be, and raced all the way round and all the way back, doing about a mile a minute, I shouldn't wonder. I thought how pleased Miss Brewer would be if she could have seen me.

"There you are, Polly! You can do it, when you make the effort."

I felt inspired to compose the following lines of poetry:

Fear makes you run like the wind,
Faster than ever before!
Fear puts joy in your heart,
While to run round the field is a bore.

I wasn't quite sure about the joy in your heart bit, but I just happened to like the sound of it and so I decided that it was poetic licence. I went up to my room and wrote the poem in my diary, directly under JESSAMY JONES'S PARTY. I thought that when I was middle-aged I would look back and remember how I had rushed round the park with Bundle, terrified of being seen.

We didn't have a Gang of Four meeting that afternoon as all of the others were off doing things. Keri was at some horsey show with Mima, Lily had a dance exam, and Frizz was helping on the Cakes &

Biscuits stall at her school fete. She'd wanted me to go along and I'd said that I might, but when the time came I was too nervous. I knew that Chantal's cousin went to Heathfield, and Chloë lived quite close, and I imagined bumping into them and having to quickly gabble about how I hadn't gone to my gran's after all.

It is so stupid to tell these sorts of lies! It just makes your life a misery. Frizz rang up later, wanting to know where I was and why I hadn't visited her stall, so with my hand over my mouth I hissed down the phone at her, "I was supposed to be at my gran's."

"You what?" said Frizz.

"*I was supposed to be at my gran's*... It was the only way I could think to get out of Jessamy Jones's beastly party!"

Chloë told me on Monday that in fact it had been quite a good party. Samantha, after all, hadn't bothered to turn up, and they had all had a lot of fun. I didn't care! I was still glad I hadn't gone.

The following Saturday it was Keri's bash, and I was really looking forward to that. Mum had at last relented and taken me into town after school on Thursday to buy me something to wear. She is not totally hard-hearted! I think she realised that Keri's party was going to be a big occasion and she didn't want me to feel like Cinderella. She knew that Keri would be dressed to kill, and she must have noticed, just lately, that Frizz had suddenly become all fashion-conscious.

So I bought a vest top – white, with a sequin patch – a pair of khaki trousers and some combat shoes.

Mum was doubtful and said, "For a party?" She wanted me to buy something pretty. "Like that little dress!" Pointing to this horrible thing hanging on a rack. All frilly and pukey and pink.

I said, "Mum! Nobody wears stuff like that."

"So why do they bother to stock it?" said Mum.

"Well, I suppose maybe if you were still at Juniors," I said.

Mum just shook her head, as if the ways of twelve-year-olds were beyond her.

When Dad saw me all dressed up in my lovely new gear he said, "That's a bit butch, isn't it?"

"She is butch," said Craig.

I said, "Shut up, or I'll bash you!"

"Oh! Oh!" Craig put up his fists and began dancing round me, daring me to have a go. I kicked out, like they do in kick boxing, and caught him on the shin. Craig yelled, "Man-hater!"

"Hooter Voice!"

"Pancake!"

"*Frog!*"

Dad was looking a bit bemused, like he couldn't quite believe his children would shout such things at each other. It was Mum, rushing in, who snapped, "Stop that, the pair of you!"

I said, "He started it! He said I was butch!"

"Craig, I'm warning you," said Mum.

Craig said, "She's a man-hater! She just kicked me on the shin. And she's really upset poor old Knickers! He fancies her like crazy and she just sneers at him."

"I do not!" I said. "I take absolutely *no notice* of him."

"You could at least smile," said Craig, "or say hello."

"That would be encouraging him. I don't want to encourage him!"

"Doesn't mean you have to look like a *gargoyle.*"

"If he doesn't like the way I look, why does he have to keep ogling me?"

Craig shouted, "'Cos he's in love and he doesn't know any better!"

I felt my cheeks fire up. Dad said, "Well, there you are, young lady! You're an object of someone's desire. Let's get you off to that party. You can inflame a few more hearts while you're there…a few more poor unsuspecting lads!"

"Not going to be any lads," I muttered, as I followed Dad out to the car.

"No lads? And you all dressed up to the nines?" said Dad. "That's a bit of a waste!"

He said it again, when we picked Frizz up. Frizz was wearing her cropped jeans and a new top. She had washed her hair and twizzled it into loops, which she had fastened with glittery hair clips shaped like stars. Well cool! But I was feeling quite cool myself, so I wasn't jealous.

"Off you go, then!" said Dad, tipping us out of the car. "Have fun! Pity about the boys."

"What did he mean?" whispered Frizz, as we made our way into the hall where Keri was having her bash.

I was about to explain, how Dad thought it was a waste for us to get all dressed up when there weren't going to be any boys – when I stopped. Because there *were* boys. Loads of them! I cringed. If Dad hadn't already driven off, I think I would have turned and run straight back to the car. Instead, I slipped my arm through Frizz's and clutched at her really tight. We'd got to stay together! So long as we stayed together, it would be all right.

Well! For about the first ten minutes we stuck like limpets. The party hadn't yet properly got going. The DJ had just arrived and was still setting up, while Keri was rushing about saying hello to people and being given her prezzies. (I'd got her a CD of Point Break. Frizz had got her a poster, also of Point Break, as just at the moment they were one of Keri's fave groups.)

"Where's Lily?" I said.

"Over there." Frizz pointed.

"Let's go and talk to her."

What I was thinking was, there's safety in numbers. If Frizz and me *and* Lily stuck together, we would be immune to boys! They couldn't get at us. I knew we couldn't expect Keri to stick, 'cos it was her party and she wanted to be the centre of attention, and anyway she was the one that had invited them. All those boys! Also there were her friends from school. I could see old Loud Mouth Mima, for instance. She was already draped over a boy. Mima was boy mad!

Frizz and me made our way across the hall, still arm in arm, to where we had caught sight of Lily, but by the time we got there, lo and behold! She had gone skipping off somewhere else.

"Where is she now?" I wailed.

"*There.*"

"Where?"

"Over there!"

Would you believe it? Lily was now on the opposite side of the hall, where we had just come from! She flits about like a sprite. It's impossible to pin her down.

"Oh, well, never mind," I said. "It'll just be you and me. Let's go and—" I broke off, somewhat alarmed. A *boy* was coming over to us. And Frizz was beaming at him!

Frizz said, "Hi!"

The boy said "Hi" back.

Frizz said, "This is my friend, Polly."

I said, "Hi."

The boy said, "Hi."

Frizz said, "This is Darren. He's in my class at school. We do cookery together." Then she added, "He's the one that taught me how to swim!"

I didn't know what to say to that so I just said, "Oh."

After that there was a bit of a silence, and then for some reason Frizz giggled.

"Good party," said the boy.

Frizz giggled again. "It's hardly started yet!"

"No, but when it does…it looks like it'll be a good one."

"Yes, it probably will be," agreed Frizz.

Then we had some more silence. I find silence really embarrassing. I cleared my throat and said, "Are you a friend of Keri's?"

"No, he's *my* friend," said Frizz. "I invited him... you know? Keri said that I could. You could probably have invited Craig if you wanted."

Invite Craig??? Was she mad???

"Look," said Frizz, "here's Lily." She unlinked her arm from mine as Lily came darting over.

"Pollee! Come!" Lily grabbed at me. "There's someone who's dying to say hello to you!"

"Who?" I said.

"Over here...quick!"

She tugged me off across the hall. I went reluctantly, 'cos I had this feeling Lily was up to mischief. She had this impish grin on her face and her eyes were all bright and gleaming. Who could it be? Who would want to say hello to me?

Heavens! Help! It was Knickers!

I screeched to a halt, glowing red like a tomato. Knickers stood there, glowing like another tomato.

"Here she is!" said Lily, pushing me at him.

"Polly." Keri came bustling up, all full of self-importance. "This is Nick. He lives just up the road from me. We've known each other for years! But he didn't know that I knew you. Did you?"

Nick shook his head.

"He knows your brother," said Keri. "They go to the same school. You could have brought him with you, if you'd wanted. Craig, I mean. We're two boys short! I d—" She stopped. "Yes, yes! I'm coming!" She waved at someone across the room. "Gotta go! Enjoy yourselves!"

Keri went racing off. So, to my horror, did Lily. Me and Knickers were left on our own. What were we going to talk about???

"Would you like me to drop dead?" he said.

I was so startled I said, "What?"

"Drop dead. I would if I could. Or I could dig a big hole and fall into it. I'm sorry! I didn't know she was going to go and drag you over. I just said I knew you; that was all. But I could go and shut myself in a cupboard. If you'd like me to. You only have to say!"

I wanted to be cross. I *was* cross. But when I opened my mouth to speak, a giggle came bursting out of me. Well, it was partly a giggle and partly a squeak. A sort of…squiggle, I suppose.

Knickers did a giggle of his own, except that boys

don't giggle in the same way girls do. His was more like a cross between a giggle and a chuckle. A chiggle. I squiggled, and he chiggled.

"I'm glad you didn't bring Craig," he said.

I said, "Why's that?"

"He keeps taking the mickey."

I said, "Yes, he does out of me, too!"

"I wanted to talk to you at the swimming baths," said Nick. Knickers. "But you didn't seem to know who I was, so I didn't like to."

Earnestly I explained to him about being short-sighted.

He said, "Me, too! But I wear contacts."

"*Oh*!" I said. "I wish I could!"

"I only just started to," he said.

"I'm going to just as soon as I can! Mum says at the moment I'm not sensible enough."

"That's what mine used to say."

"She says I'd take Bundle up the park and start playing around and they'd fall out and I'd lose them."

"Mum said the same about me playing football."

"Do you play football a lot?" I said. I'd just been starting to get this fellow-feeling going, what with us both being short-sighted and his mum saying to him all the things that my mum said to me. Now I supposed he was going to tell me he was a mad sports freak. "Which team d'you support?"

"Um – well." He looked a bit shamefaced. "I don't really support any...not specially. I'm not terribly into it, to tell you the truth. We have to play at school, of course."

"Like us," I said. "We have to play *hockey*." I pulled a face. So did Nick. "And sometimes," I said, "they make us *run* all round the playing field."

"Yeah! We have to do that. We've got this one teacher, Mr Hatwell, we call him Hitwell, he keeps coming after us, yelling and bawling like a lunatic."

I cried, "We've got one the same! Miss Brewer. She's *brutal!* It's not that I don't like exercise," I said. "But it has to be the right sort of exercise. Like, taking Bundle out, that's OK!"

"You don't think..." Nick had gone very red. Redder than tomato. Red like he was about to burst. "You don't think..." he said it all in one big rush – "you-don't-think-I-could-come-and-take-Bundle-out-with-you-one-day-do-you?"

Well! What could I say? It would have been hurtful to say no. And I couldn't immediately think of any excuse. Afterwards I thought I could have said that Bundle only liked walking with me, on my own; or that I liked to be by myself so that I could make up poems in my head. But I didn't, so we made this arrangement that he would call round next day and we would go up the park together.

"But not with Craig," I said.

We both agreed: not with Craig!

Later on, towards the end of the party, after we'd played lots of games and done a bit of dancing, I found myself in the cloakroom with the others.

"We saw!" giggled Lily. "We saw you…huddled in the corner!"

"Yes," added Frizz, "and we saw who you were huddled with!"

"Am I forgiven now?" said Keri.

"For what?" I said.

"Inviting *boys*!"

"Heavens!" I said. Cool as could be. "It's your party! You can invite who you like."

"I thought you'd be mad at me," said Keri.

"What, for inviting boys?" I did this little laugh. More of a trill, really. Like, how amusing! "There's nothing wrong with boys," I said. "Girls are more groovy, but boys are OK."

Well, some of them!

I had a kind of feeling that this time next year I

might be going to owe Gran a whole week's worth of telephone calls… But I knew that whatever happened, however OK boys turned out to be (some of them!), I'd still be friends with Keri, and Lily, and Frizz.

I pictured how it might be, in the future… Lily, of course, would be a dancer. There wasn't any doubt about that! She'd be famous the world over, and we'd all go to see her, and visit her afterwards in her dressing room. And she'd still be just the same as she was now, 'cos fame wouldn't change her one little bit. She wouldn't get grand, or big-headed. She'd still be Lily!

Frizz would be a chef and own her own restaurant. A veggie one. *Cordon vert*. Five stars in the restaurant guides! She would probably get married to another chef and they would have lots of children. I could see Frizz with lots of children. I thought that she would make a very good mother. She'd love them to bits and never be mean or crotchety with them. But she'd still run the restaurant, and we'd all go and eat there. We'd meet there once a year, and giggle and gossip and remember when we were young.

Even Keri! Who would be busy as could be, leading this mad social life. I thought Keri would probably do some swanky sort of job, like in the City, and would marry a man who was immensely rich and powerful. A banker, or an MP, or something. They'd have a house in the country and another one in town and there would be pictures of them in those glossy sort of magazines that you find in the dentist's. And when she turned up for our meeting she would always come by cab, and she would sweep in like she owned the place, even though it would be Frizz who owned it and Lily who was the famous one. But that's Keri for you!

She wouldn't change, any more than Lily.

As for me, I thought I would probably just bumble along doing my own thing, whatever that might turn out to be. I didn't think I would ever be famous, or rich, or have my picture in glossy magazines. But I might get married and I might have children and I would certainly have a dog! Maybe lots of dogs. And some cats, too, and maybe a donkey in the back garden. And I wouldn't envy any of the others because I would be quite happy just being me.

The important thing was, we would still be the Gang of Four. Friends for ever! Just like always. Keri and Lily, and Frizz and me.

About the Author

Jean Ure had her first book published while she was still at school and immediately went rushing out into the world declaring that she was AN AUTHOR. But it was another few years before she had her second book published, and during that time she had to work at lots of different jobs to earn money. In the end she went to drama school to train as an actress. While she was there she met her husband and wrote another book. She has now written more than eighty books! She lives in Croydon with her husband and their family of seven rescued dogs and four rescued cats.

£3.99   1 84121 835 9

What will happen when the Gang of Four
move to new schools?
Will they be able to stick together then?
And will they get rid of Jessamy James,
who wears pink knickers and is just so uncool?

**Polly is in for a surprise
at her new school...**

£3.99   1 84121 839 1

The girlfriends are all going to different schools now.
The gang meets every Saturday, but suddenly
Polly finds she has other invitations, like to her
new friend, Chloë's, party.

Who will Polly choose?
Will the girlfriends stick together?

£3.99 1 84121 843 X

Frizz is behaving very strangely.
     Polly is worried that Frizz hates her new
school and feels lonely without the
                    rest of the Gang of Four.

But is Frizz feeling left out,
          or is she the grooviest girl of all?

More Orchard Red Apples

All Girlfriends books priced at £3.99, all others £4.99

Orchard Red Apples are available from all good
bookshops,
or can be ordered direct from the publisher:
Orchard Books, PO BOX 29, Douglas IM99 1BQ
Credit card orders please telephone 01624 836000
or fax 01624 837033
or e-mail: bookshop@enterprise.net for details.

To order please quote title, author and ISBN
and your full name and address.
Cheques and postal orders should be made payable to
'Bookpost plc.'
Postage and packing is FREE within the UK
(overseas customers should add £1.00 per book).

Prices and availability are subject to change